Successful businessman Yvan Routhier has
extensive working experience in business management and
corporate development. Over the years, he acquired a
strong expertise in bank financing (both as lender and
borrower), in M&A (Mergers and Acquisitions), as well as
projects analysis. He is recognized for his interpersonal
qualities, negotiating skills, and immediate adaption to
different environments, making them more efficient,
functional, and equitable. Trilingual; he speaks French,
English, and Spanish. Today, he is involved in a number of
business startups and devotes his personal time to writing,
as well as trading stock options and cryptocurrencies.

Copyright © 2021 Yvan Routhier

Contents

Prologue

Standing at her bedroom window, staring into the night sky, was a gloomy Sophia. Lost in her thoughts, she sighed and looked out of the window at the empty street. Sophia wasn't always like this; it was pretty evident that she had something on her mind, something that was bothering her a lot. One could tell it was probably a heartbreak.

She desperately began searching for ways to gather herself in her thoughts but gave up and wrapped her arms around her in an attempt to embrace herself, hoping to find the slightest bit of comfort. Unfortunately, all her efforts continued to go in vain. She couldn't get him out of her head and, more importantly, her heart. It was as if he was etched in her soul, not just her life. Her days and nights were all the same, spent in despair. Everything reminded her of him, and somehow, she even felt his presence, but she still longed for him to magically appear out of her thoughts, right back into her life.

She knew it was wrong, but she couldn't help herself; even though Sophia had heard rumors about his marriage, but despite all her efforts, her heart still desired him. After all this time, she still couldn't accept otherwise. She couldn't stop thinking about him and was missing him irrepressibly. All she craved was his touch again. As she began to reminisce, she caressed her arms, took a deep breath in, and held herself tight, hoping she'd feel as she once did in his arms.

With her eyes shut tight, all she wanted to do at that moment was to hold herself and think about him. She went back to the times she had spent with him, locked in his embrace when she could feel his skin on hers, and he'd look into her eyes and smile at her. Just thinking about it, she felt as if she was taken somewhere else. Sophia felt a strange sense of comfort in quixotically imagining him; she breathed a sigh of relief but still didn't seem to cheer up as she walked toward her bedroom door and turned to lock it.

She hoped to feel the same comfort again, even if it wasn't exactly her ideal fantasy since those revolved around entirely different circumstances where he'd still be a part of her life, holding her close and promising never to let go. Either way, she kept on caressing her arms and embracing herself and shutting her eyes, all ready to step into her dreams, which were the only place she'd get to feel him again. She pictured him smiling and walking toward her as she ran into his arms and clung onto him as if she'd never let him go. Sophia could feel the goosebumps on her skin as she continued to try and dream him into life. She yearned to be held by him, wanted by him; she couldn't get over his touch or forget how his lips felt on hers and on every part of her body. She felt her heart beat faster as she imagined him leaning in to kiss her, she gasped as she felt the intensity building up and her heart racing when suddenly....

"Sophia? Are you in there, Sophia?"

She heard her mother call her from outside the door. And just like that, she was back to life, the life where she dreaded reality more and more each day.

Sophia walked toward the door to open it.

"What is it?" she asked. The disappointment and anger on her face were evident.

"This parcel arrived for you," replied her mother, as she held out the package.

Sophia grabbed the box irritably and looked at it from all sides, trying to find the sender's label.

"Who sent it?" Sophia asked.

"It doesn't say, but the courier man specifically said it was for you," her mother replied.

Silence filled the room as they both stared at the parcel in Sophia's hand.

"It can't be a bomb, can it?" Sophia asked jokingly.

Her mother shook her head amusingly and turned around.

"Silly, I'll leave you to it. Come down for dinner soon. It's been long since you ate with us," added her mother.

"I'll think about it."

"Does that mean you won't be joining us?" asked her mother.

"No, it means that I'll think about whether to join or not and then I'll decide."

"When does this deciding period end, Sophia?" her mother asked, with pleading eyes.

"Tomorrow morning," replied Sophia, without much thought.

"Sophia…," said her mother, as she reached out her hand and tried to reason with her.

"Not today, Mother, not today," Sophia replied as she turned around and went into her room.

She shut the door, leaned her back against it, and heard her mother's footsteps fading. She felt guilty for shutting everyone out, but she had also convinced herself that there was nothing else she could do. She told herself that she was in this alone, and she didn't want her wretchedness to wear off on the people around her, especially the ones she loved and genuinely cared for.

She sat down, looked around, and felt a feeling of emptiness taking over her. She clenched her lips and inhaled sharply while her eyes teared up.

"Not today," she whispered again to herself.

Chapter One

Sophia stormed out of the coffee shop in a cloak of fury and onto the sidewalk. Walking past her car, she jammed her key into the wrong vehicle, which soon had the alarm blaring for the entire street to hear. Its owner then came out of one of the shops on the other side of the street and gently made his way to the vehicle, where Sophia stood still, slightly terrified. Her face was turning pink as she saw him approaching her. "Crap," she muttered.

Sophia stared at the man crossing the street and felt her stomach churn. "Naveen?" she whispered to herself. *What is he doing here?* she thought to herself. Looking lost, Sophia took another glance at Naveen, who was walking casually toward her, as he seemed to be in no hurry. In fact, he smiled at her and then winked. She was trying to catch her breath as she looked away, completely flustered. She brought her hands to her face and tried to calm herself down. Her palms were sweaty. "Oh, dear," she whispered to herself.

Naveen was then a few steps from her. She evidently mistook his car for hers. She certainly needed to hide her feelings for him and play hard to get.

"What is it?" she asked, trying to sound angry and avoiding his eyes.

"You're avoiding me," Naveen said in a slightly angered tone.

She somehow tried to move away, but he placed both hands at either side of the car, trapping her.

"Let me go, Naveen. What are you doing here?"

She tried pushing him, but he leaned in closer, dangerously close, his cologne making her dizzy. She gulped and blinked rapidly.

"Why are you avoiding me, Sophia?"

"I'm not avoiding you."

Her salivary gland seemed to stop working, and her brain felt like it was about to shut down.

"I'm not avoiding you," she said again.

"Then, why are you acting like this? You're not answering my calls, you're not replying to any of my messages, and the last time I called, you even told your friend Corinne to lie for you.

She looked away. His accusations were true, but that Corinne part, she had no hand in it; her friend was only being loyal to her.

"Then, I was probably sleeping," Sophia simply said.

"Really?" he asked. "Why then is your eyelid twitching? You do this when you're lying," he blurted.

She squeezed her eyes shut. *Shoot, this man knows I have Pinocchio syndrome,* she thought to herself.

"Fine, I…wasn't exactly sleeping, but…just let me go," she said. He had let his guard down, so she could easily push him away.

"Come with me." He proposed, after a brief silence, trying to pull her along with him.

"I'm not going anywhere with you!" she said. "And I just can't leave my car here, so far from work."

"I'll call my driver to come and pick it up." Naveen proposed. She shook her head; the offer was tempting, but she didn't want to go anywhere with him and again have the paparazzi all over her face the next day. Corinne had shown her a picture of the two of them that once appeared in the newspaper when they were together, and that idiot still wondered why she would avoid being seen in public with him. Especially now as they were not 'a thing.'

"I'm not going, Naveen; I'm not," she replied, looking up at him.

He had the most mysterious eyes, glossy brown with a flickering hint of green. They were so beautiful she could get lost in them. But they darkened silvery darkness of despair at her response. He furrowed his eyebrows and took a deep breath.

"Sophia, we need to talk." He tried again.

"I don't have anything to say to you," she replied, folding her arms stubbornly.

"Fine, have dinner with me."

"No luck, Naveen, not today."

"Tomorrow, then?"

"No!" She half yelled. "Some other time, but not today."

She opened her car door. Looking defeated, he tried to straighten himself.

"Why aren't you at work?"

"I took the day off," she said as she started the engine. "See you in another life, Naveen."

"Bye," he murmured, through his white gritted teeth, as he watched her drive off.

Corinne looked up from her store's counter and frowned slightly. "You're here? Weren't you supposed to go home?"

Sophia stormed past her into the office behind. Corinne looked at her assistant in confusion.

"Leela, watch this place for me, will you? I'll be back. The goddess of fury and unhappiness must have paid Sophia a visit this month."

"Tell me about it," Leela said, giggling.

Corinne opened the door and shut it gently behind her. She looked at Sophia seated, arm draped across her forehead, as she seemed to have fallen asleep. "Don't play possum with me, Sophia." With that, Sophia opened her eyes. "Alright, spill it, I'm listening."

"I'm tired; I just want to die," Sophia said, without thinking and shutting her eyes again.

"Sweet Lord! What's gotten into you?" replied Corinne. "Are you even listening to yourself? Look, just calm down and tell me what happened."

"Don't tell me to calm down; you know it doesn't work like that. I just…." Sophia put her hands up in defeat and stood up. "I don't know." She held her head, pushing a lock of hair away from her face.

"You need a break," Corinne said with an understanding smile.

"I need an aspirin," Sophia replied. She grabbed the container from a shelf and a plastic cup by the dispenser. Chucking it into her mouth, she drank the water, spilling some on herself. Breathing hard, she looked deranged.

"First, there is my mom. She didn't think of at least talking to me before she got married to that…that man," Sophia started saying, flinging the cup away.

"He's your stepfather Sophia…."

"Hell no! Don't you call him my stepfather; he's my mother's husband. My. Mother's. Husband!" Sophia chewed each word before blurting it out.

"They look happy together."

"Does it look like I care?" Sophia ranted with a frown.

"Don't be selfish, Bill."

"That's it, that's the problem. My mom no longer bears Bill; I'm the only one who has something linked with my dad."

"Sophia…."

"And my sister. She seems to be all over him, going all dad, dad, dad. Dad did this; Dad said that, Dad! Ugh."

Corinne rolled her eyes and shook her head.

"Then, today, Naveen showed up out of nowhere."

"Pretty boy showed up, huh?" Corinne said, with a teasing note, not paying much attention to the rest that Sophia had said.

"What did he say?"

"Many things. He knows I'm avoiding him."

"He's so smart."

Sophia gave her a smug look. "Then, he wanted me to go with him, have dinner with him, can you believe that?" she added dramatically.

"How romantic. Did you agree?" Corinne asked.

"It's official; you're crazy! I didn't. I can't wake up again to the media camping outside my door tomorrow."

"Come on, cut him some slack!"

"Says the one who lied on my behalf."

"You won't." Corinne laughed in disbelief.

"Of course, I won't."

Sophia sat down, exhausted. Her blonde-haired friend came and bent before her.

"Sweetheart, you need a vacation. Take a week off; I'll handle your boutique for you. Leela can take care of things for me around here."

"No, I don't think I do," Sophia said.

"Neither do I," Corinne replied. Sophia gave her a strange look.

"Listen, I don't think you need a vacation. I know you need a vacation."

Sophia opened her mouth to protest.

"No ifs or buts! I'll make the bookings; you just go home, rest, and pack your bags," Corinne added.

"What would I do without you, Corinne?" Sophia asked, thankfully, while hugging her.

"Everything except having someone to talk to. Now get going and check your mailbox tomorrow morning," Corinne replied as she smiled at her.

"Where are you sending me to?" Sophia asked, standing up, looking very confused and borderline excited.

"Perhaps it is Rome, or maybe somewhere in Italy. You will see," Corinne replied with a mischievous grin. "Or maybe Vienna…why not fight fire with fire? You once were over there with Naveen; maybe you should make it back there by yourself and finally get him out of your system!"

"I'm crazy, I know."

Sophia shook her head as she opened the door, thinking Corinne was messing around with her while thinking her idea of going back to Vienna was not so bad after all.

"I love you too, girl!" Corinne called out after her, bobbing up and down in her sneakers.

"Vacation mode activated. Vienna, here we come!" Sophia exclaimed.

Chapter Two

Naveen was sitting in his swivel chair in his study and kept looking at the clock as it ticked away. Tapping the huge mahogany table with a pen out of what seemed like anticipation, he picked up his phone and dialed his home number.

"Frances, please don't bother cooking dinner; I'll be eating out tonight."

Whomever he spoke to must have reprimanded him about the lateness and eating out, which made him smile as he said, "I know it's late, Frances. I'll eat a vegetarian dish, something I can easily digest. Thanks for being concerned about my health, just like always."

There was a pause, then Naveen asked, "Did she come over? No? Alright. I'll see you soon. Please shut the doors and turn the lights off. I'll just use my key to come in."

The call ended, and he sighed. He stood up and picked his keys while giving the room a quick glance.

"Why are you doing this to me, Sophia? Why? I'm not in my right mind, and it's all because of you. I can't think straight, and everything bothers me, all because of you." He sighed again.

He stepped out into the chilliness of the evening breeze and nodded goodnight to the gatekeeper as he drove away from the industrial area where his head office was located. Rather than having dinner in a restaurant, as he had told Frances, he headed for a bar close to the old part of the city. Being a regular, he knew the place well and thought it best, given the mood he was in. He didn't feel like talking to anyone or, for that matter, be entertained. Once inside, he took a seat, and one of the waiters he had known for years came to him.

"Georges, did you receive this rum from the Dominican Republic that we already talked about?"

The waiter, who knew his collection of exotic beverages by heart, was delighted he could finally open the first bottle of this new arrival.

"We did, Sir," he replied. He was back with the fine drink within moments.

Naveen looked at his watch and saw that it was eight o'clock sharp. He smirked and looked around. There were a few people, which he thought was good, as he could spend some time thinking without anyone noticing his presence or getting in his way. But what was there to think about? The business was doing fine. One of his franchisees had called in the morning to let him know of an increase in the number of units sold, as there was a higher demand for the company's products, which meant more revenue (always a good thing). He thought about the oak barrels coming in that week, which was a new strategy they were working on to add a finer taste to certain wines they were distributing. He smiled bitterly and thought to himself how funny it was that he owned a wine business, and here he

was drinking liquor at a bar; he thought of it as an irony!

"Oh, Sophia, the things you do to me...."

His smile soon faded as Sophia wasn't the only

headache he had, a nice headache though he thought it was.

Even though Sophia was still always on his mind, after all

this time, and she'd literally conquered all his thoughts,

which sometimes led to cloudy judgment and absent-

mindedness, she wasn't the only reason. There were clearly

other things going on. His wife was his major problem, or

better put it, his ex-wife. Funny how a person can leave

your life, but the issues you had with them still remain.

Again, ironic. He downed his rum, which he enjoyed, and

asked Georges for another one. It turned out he would go

for more than just another one.

Dragging prenuptial agreement issues between the

two of them at the moment was the last thing he needed. Of

course, if he were to have it his way, he wouldn't deal with it at all. She was financially stable and didn't need the money. Yet, she took delight in tormenting him for some unknown reason. She made it her duty to rob him of any peace of mind at every slightest opportunity that presented itself to her. The other day, she showed up at his doorstep waving papers with a wicked look on her face.

"I'm pregnant!" She piqued.

He tried hard to contain his laughter but ended up laughing anyway. Not at the news, but because she had so much makeup on, he thought she looked like a cartoon, which is why he burst out laughing uncontrollably.

"You're talking rubbish," he said, then asked, "How far along are you?"

"Three," she replied.

He was stunned! Suddenly, it felt as if he was given a terrible reality check. He gaped at her, not knowing how else to react. Was she even listening to herself? They had been divorced for two months, and he hadn't touched her for at least three months before that, which made it entirely impossible for what she now seemed to be claiming.

"You know what, Drizella? You're sick. Very sick! You take these papers to whomever the rando is that got you pregnant. You're looking in the wrong house."

"Rando!" She looked like an ostrich ready to fight. "And this, coming from the man who was caught with his pants down having sex with his wife's friend!" She attacked.

"That was a long time ago, Drizella!"

"Oh, really? It seems like yesterday to me. I'm not trash like you! I'd never stoop so low," she said, waving her hand across the air for a more dramatic effect.

"What is wrong with you, Ella?" he asked, flaring up at being reminded of that unfortunate mistake which he'd been trying hard to forget, even though nothing about that mistake could ever bring bad memories.

"I want half of the assets, as they should belong to me and everything else that we agreed upon."

He sized her up and decided she wasn't worth the argument.

"You're not getting anything from me. Not a single thing!" he said as he shut the door at her face.

She yelled something about hearing from her lawyer, but he didn't seem to care. Moments later, she was driving off as if possessed by the devil.

He turned his drink in his hand and belched.

"Pregnant," he muttered. "Stupid."

He knew he couldn't handle the alcohol he was drinking, yet he finished the drink he was having. He picked up his phone and called his friend. His speech was slurred since the liquor had already started to kick in, and Naveen didn't feel like himself very much whenever he was tipsy.

"Hey Rick, how are you doing? Is this a good time?" he asked.

"Yes and no. Is everything okay?" came the reply.

"Mind picking me up? Don't think I can drive myself."

"Are you drunk?"

"A little bit," Naveen said, twirling the content of his glass.

"Where are you exactly?"

"Breezy's."

There was a brief silence at the other end, then the call ended. Moments later, Naveen was staggering beside his friend, headed for his car.

"It's the end of the world!" he sang, tottering here and there.

Rick staggered while trying to drag him along. "How many glasses did you have?"

"About five or six, maybe seven or eight; does it matter? It's the end of the world!" he yelled again.

"Will you stop yelling? You're drawing attention, and that's the last thing we need right now," replied Rick.

He opened the back door and shoved Naveen in, catching his breath out of exhaustion dragging his friend, who by then barely had any control over his body.

"Is it Christmas already?" Naveen asked with a silly face. Clearly, he wasn't going to sober up anytime soon.

Rick rolled his baby eyes and shook his head. *Naveen must've been really messed up about something,* Rick thought, *or else he wouldn't ever be in this state. Naveen isn't the irresponsible type to just get drunk out of nowhere.*

"No, Santa Claus, we're in July; Christmas isn't for another five months. What happened to you, Naveen? You never drink!"

"Why is it snowing in here then?" Being surprised would have been an understatement; Rick was stupefied.

"Was your drink spiked with something, or were you with someone?"

"Yes." Naveen groaned. "Problems. My drink was laced with a concoction of all the problems a man could ever think of."

Rick started the car and said nothing. The ride home was silent, as Naveen snored like a drunk elephant while Rick thought about what to do with his friend in that particular situation.

He rang the doorbell and waited till someone opened it. It was Frances.

"Rick? You're here?" asked Frances, motioning toward the car. "Naveen? Is he drunk?" she asked.

"Very drunk, unfortunately," said Rick.

"But he told me he was going to eat out tonight. Looks like he went and drank himself to a stupor." The elderly woman sighed. "Let's take him upstairs."

"Sure." Rick turned and went to open the door.

With his arms draped across Frances's and Rick's shoulders, Naveen opened his eyes a little bit. He muttered something incoherent and drooped his head to raise it again.

"Mother? Is that you, Mother?" he muttered.

"No, it's Frances," Rick answered.

"Who's Frances?" he asked as they opened the door to his room.

"Your housekeeper!" Rick grunted as they both collapsed onto the king-sized bed.

"Oh, hey, housekeeper," Naveen said, waving to Frances. "My head hurts a lot; I might need a drink."

Frances smiled sadly.

"I'll prepare some ginger tea; you've already had enough to drink," she replied before turning around and disappearing.

"Make some ginger grass instead," Naveen said, calling after her.

"Ginger grass, I think you mean lemongrass?" Rick asked.

"You know what I mean! Don't bother me, Rick."

Rick stood up and planted his hands on his hips as he looked down at Naveen, shaking his head.

"So now I'm bothering you, huh?"

"That's not what I meant; you know that."

"Take a break, Naveen. Go on a vacation and offload the stress. You need it. Away from all these troubles and drama before you completely lose it."

There was a prolonged silence, and for a moment, Rick thought Naveen had fallen asleep. He continued when he realized he was still awake, trying to find a more comfortable sleeping position. "You have a house in Vienna, don't you? Take some time out, go unwind. Stay as long as you need to get better."

Frances came in, bringing the mug silently.

"Sit up and have your tea, Naveen. And I do think you need the holiday I'm talking about."

"If you insist," Naveen replied as he sat up, holding his forehead in his palm.

Maybe I do need a holiday, he thought. *At least, my lunatic wife would be out of my hair for some time.*

"I'll leave tomorrow morning," Naveen finally said, giving Rick a reassuring squeeze.

"I'll book the flight for you," Rick said, looking at his watch. "I'll leave now. My wife is calling. See you later, Naveen; goodnight, Frances."

"Rick!" Naveen called out. "Thanks a bunch."

"Anytime," replied Rick, smiling at him.

"Ladies and gentlemen, please switch off your phones and fasten your seatbelts; the plane is about to take off."

From his business class seat (he never flew first class, not worth the money), Naveen came out of his musings and took in his surroundings. He picked up his phone and sent a message to Rick: "We're about to take off; will call when I arrive in Vienna."

Slightly behind him in the economy class, Sophia did the same as she was about to put her phone on flight mode. Having no occupied seats behind her, she thought, later on, she could recline hers and put on a sleeping mask. She might as well sleep through the whole flight since she'd been up all night, restless. She was so tempted to call him, but she was determined not to. She had decided that neither would she call him nor would she answer his calls even though she anticipated hearing from him.

Her phone rang, and she rushed to answer, but it was a call from Corrine instead, far from who she expected (or was hoping for). She ignored the call, folded her arms, and tried really hard to get some sleep, but she just couldn't stop thinking about him; his beautiful face, his melodious voice with a slight Spanish accent, which made her love him even more, his delicate hands feeling her skin.

She longed to feel him again, to have him touch her face gently and smile at her. Every time he would kiss her, she would then feel her senses simply disappear as if she was out of this world. At that moment, she was playing back the images of how he couldn't seem to keep his hands off her body and the way he sounded when he called out her name while making love to her. She missed him, it was evident, but she wished she didn't miss him, or his touch for that matter. However hard she tried not to think about him, everything somehow went back to him, and there he'd be again, right in her head and her heart.

Sophia felt like she was in love back then and that nothing could undo the two, but now, backed in reality, she felt her heart hurting.

How unlucky does one have to be to lose the one they love? She thought to herself. Sophia was a focused person, but her attention span was as short as Naveen's temper. Even though her mind wandered to a hundred different places while thinking about anything related to work or her routine when it came to him, her mind seemed to stay exactly where it was and continued to playback all their times together. They'd made memories; they weren't years' worth of memories, but that didn't make her treasure them any less. She just seemed to go on and on about how he made her feel; it was as if it had taken over her.

She shook her head to clear out the imagery; she knew she would go mad if it continued. She plugged in the earphones to listen to some music, but he was there too, even in the songs from her playlist. Above all, she had this strong feeling he was close, so close, she could feel him. She opened her eyes and looked around her, but the faces were not familiar. "I'm now imagining things," she said to herself in a whisper while resting her head back.

Naveen's head shot up from his chair; he thought he heard her voice, rather faint, but he could swear he heard it. He shook his head, laughing at himself.

Don't be weird, Naveen; there's no way she'll be here! He thought. *Or could she?*

As he waived that thought, picking up a magazine, he saw something that caught his attention in the index and flipped to the article. It was an interview that he had had a month ago about his wine company, Silver Moon. He smiled with satisfaction; with the way things were going, he was convinced his company would need more branches internationally. He had given several interviews, but none of them would compare with this one.

A hostess passed by with a trolley of food and stopped beside him. Smiling so sweetly, she batted her eyelids in a flirting way.

"Tea or coffee?" she asked in a singing voice.

"Coffee, please. Thanks," he said courteously, ignoring her body language.

She took his order and bent low enough for him alone to hear.

"Let me know if you need anything," she whispered and straightened.

You didn't need to be voodoo to understand what she meant.

"No, thanks, I'm good," he replied politely and then nodded, raising his cup of coffee.

"Alright, then." She had put on her professional mask again, not really feeling the slightest bit of embarrassment, and went to tend to someone else.

He reclined into his seat and waited, counting the hours as they passed, a part of him feeling hopeful.

"A few hours, Naveen, just a few, and you'll be far away from Drizella and all her troubles, and you will start feeling better again. And away from Sophia as well. He reflected himself grimly. *But do I really want to be away from Sophia?* he thought to himself.

He pursed his lips, shut his eyes, and fell asleep. When he opened them again, he realized he was being tapped on his shoulder by an air hostess, a different one this time.

"The plane has landed, sir. Welcome to Vienna. I hope you had a lovely trip," she said to him.

"What?" His eyes felt gritty. He looked around and saw people leaving their seats, getting out of the aircraft through the various exits. "Oh yes, yes I did, thanks." He stood up and fumbled in his pockets for his phone, shaking off the sleepy state he was in, and began to feel hopeful about his vacation.

Having made it out of the plane and then the terminal without coming across Naveen, Sophia flagged down a taxi and gave the driver the address to the hotel that Corinne had booked for her. Only then, as her driver was putting her luggage in the car's trunk, did she look up and saw Naveen about to be picked up by his ride. It wasn't a taxi, so it could have been someone he knew.

Naveen? Here in Vienna? This is a joke, right? What is he doing here? How could we end up here at the same time? She thought to herself as she turned her face away and hurried into her own taxi, hoping he hadn't seen her, still half wishing he had. It was clear that both of them were in the same state of mind, wanting to be with and without each other.

"Okay, Sophia, calm down; there's no need to overreact; he didn't even see you. Just keep yourself together, and you will be fine. Stay strong because you do not need this right now; you're on vacation to get away from him, remember that." Which, at this point, suddenly seemed highly unlikely....

Oh dear, she thought to herself. The driver got in and started the car.

"Sorry, Sir, could we leave quickly and drive fast, without slowing down; again, I'm sorry, but I'm in sort of a hurry," she said frantically.

"I'm sorry, Ma'am, but there are speed limits that I have to stick to. I don't want the police breathing down our neck," the driver replied.

"Okay, fine. I'm not asking you to violate the rules; I'm just asking you to drive fast, as fast as the speed limit allows you to. Is that possible?"

"Any problem, Ma'am? Are you running from someone?" he asked back.

"Yes. No. Just go and be quick."

"But ma'am—"

"Just go, please!"

The driver eased the car out of the airport, with Sophia heaving a sigh of relief as she'd gotten away successfully without being seen.

Close call, she thought. She circled in her mind the fact that they had been on the same plane, so her hunch earlier was correct; he was physically close, really close. She couldn't believe she was right; the odds of this happening felt so unlikely.

They had only driven halfway from the airport when they heard a loud noise.

"What was that?" she asked out of fright as the vehicle came to a stop.

"I'll take a look," the driver replied as he got out of the car. He cursed under his breath as Sophia got out as well to inspect what was wrong and where the noise might come from.

"Ma'am, we have a burst tire. We're lucky the vehicle stopped so easily; it could have been way worse."

Sophia felt thirsty all of a sudden. "I do not need this right now. You do have a spare tire, don't you? Please tell me you have a spare tire?"

"I did, but I no longer do. It might be hard to get it fixed at this time; might as well get you another taxi. It is getting late, and this isn't the busiest route…let me figure something out; I obviously can't leave you here."

Sophia looked at her watch; it was, in fact, getting late. She was quite sure she had been hexed; bad luck simply followed her everywhere, even out of the country apparently.

"Need a lift?" Someone in a silver color car offered, as the auto glass was being wound down.

She didn't even have to look. It was happening. Even though she had tried as hard as she could to avoid it, it was him again. She could clearly recognize his voice. Something about bad luck as a companion; she needed the lift, so now she had to swallow her ego, no matter how much she tried not to.

"Could you put her things in the back?" Naveen asked his driver as he stepped out of the car to open the door for Sophia. She could almost see the fireworks over his head and cupid doing a happy dance. Her problem was only about to get worse because, of course, bad luck was loving Sophia today. They went around five hotels in the area, but they were all full, while none could confirm that Sophia Bill had a reservation under her name.

"But Corinne told me she had booked a room for me!" Sophia said in exasperation.

"Did she say which hotel?"

"I forgot to ask…and furthermore, I do not have any written confirmation. I am, however, darn sure it was the first one we went to."

She was exhausted and hungry. She had only one option, but she remained quiet. She simply had not seen this coming. Headline: Red alert, perfect vacation to forget about everything gone wrong!

"You certainly could come to my place. That is if it's alright with you?" Naveen suddenly declared. Of course, she wouldn't and couldn't mind, as it was clear she had no other option at that point. Even a bat could see that. She, however, kept quiet, saying nothing.

"You have to make up your mind, Sophia, as it is getting late; you should make a decision."

Again, she said nothing, arguing with herself on something that was becoming a reality.

"I'll take your silence as a yes," Naveen finally said.

"Can we at least try another hotel?" she could hear herself asking.

He raised his eyebrows, his tanned face reflecting his sense of humor.

"Really, Sophia?"

He held her hand and felt her trying to withdraw. She knew she wanted to hold his hand, but part of her didn't. And the part that did, she definitely couldn't show it.

"Come on. It's quite late. We should go," said Naveen, feeling relieved that he'd finally convinced Sophia.

"Fine," Sophia said, surrendering.

Chapter Three

The house was quite impressive and well-kept, Sophia acknowledged as they came in. She knew Naveen owned property close to Vienna, but she had never made it there with him. Instead, this one time, they did spend three days together in the city; they only visited the interior of their top floor suite at the beautiful Hotel Kärntnerhof located downtown. A stay she had never forgotten about....

"Good evening, sir. How was your trip?" Nikolai, the housekeeper, asked.

"It was alright, thank you for asking," replied Naveen, slightly nodding his head.

"Welcome back to Vienna."

The housekeeper smiled and carried the bags up the stairs. Nikolai had a rather questionable look on his face until Naveen called out. "Please show Ms. Bill to her room, Nikolai."

Sophia looked at Naveen in slight awkwardness and smiled subtly. *Nikolai*, she mused; *that explains the heavy Russian accent*, she thought to herself, smiling as he gestured with his hand for her to come with him.

As they both approached the stairs, she looked back and noticed Naveen had not moved from the door ever since they had entered. She saw him staring with a little smile on his face; it was almost as if it was victorious even. He gave her a thumbs-up. She smiled to herself and made her way up the stairs.

Sophia entered the room where Nikolai had led her. She looked around and breathed a sigh of relief and relaxation. She was quite impressed with the interior and overall look of the room – almost as if Naveen knew she'd be staying there. Sophia took a look around and turned toward the bed, which looked like heaven to her right now. All she wanted to do was slide into her comfy silk pajamas and jump into the warm and cozy bed. But before that, she wanted to freshen up a bit. She opened the door to the bathroom, and the beautiful scent of roses and lavender surrounded her. Sophia smiled because she knew she would now be having a long relaxing shower.

She turned on the hot water and stood under it for quite a while; she felt as if her stress and worries ran down her body with water flow. After a comforting shower, she put on the super-soft bathrobe and went back into the room. She loved how fresh and clean she felt. She smelled of chamomile, shea butter, and a combination of other sweet smells from all the products she had used to shower.

Sophia heard a knock on the door as she dried her hair with a towel. Afraid it may be Naveen, she tightened her bathrobe and made her way to the door. It was Nikolai bringing a tray full of hot food up to her room.

"Your dinner, Ma'am," he said politely as he held out the tray.

"Thank you," she said. As she took the tray from him, she looked at his face and noticed that he was trying to ask her something but was hesitant. "You want to say something?" she asked in an inquisitive tone.

He was hesitant, as if unsure whether to talk or not, but then he took a deep breath in and said, "Sir Naveen, he has never brought any woman here before. Well apart from his wife on their honeymoon, during which they had a fight on the second day from arriving, and after which she left him and never came back."

"Okay?" Sophia said, not fully understanding the reason behind the story but trying to be polite either way.

"Needless to say, you must be really special to him, and it is, therefore, a pleasure meeting you. You're thinking of becoming our boss's new wife, right?"

"What? Um, anyway, thanks, Nikolai; it's nice to meet you too as well. I am Sophia," she said in a hurried manner, hoping for the awkward conversation to end as soon as possible.

"You have a beautiful name," Nikolai said, smiling.

"Thanks to my parents, Nikolai," Sophia replied, as she smiled at him and leaned behind the door, slightly closing it while gesturing that she was going back inside.

He paused a little and hesitated to speak up again but then said, "You make him happy, and we haven't seen him happy in a long time, Miss. Good night." He turned around and left in a hurry, hoping he had not said too much.

"Okay," Sophia said, slightly confused. "Goodnight," she said again, closing the door gently, not fully comprehending what just had happened.

After enjoying a relaxing shower and a scrumptious meal, she yearned for a good night's sleep. She'd been restless and tired for over a week and desperately needed rest. She thought to herself that she'd call Corrine in the morning and inquire about the hotel she was supposed to have booked as there was no way she was going to continue staying here. This was going to become an emergency—a very comfortable and peaceful emergency, that is.

Did she really want to leave? She knew that's what her ego wanted and what would make her look 'hard-to-get,' but did she really want to go? She knew she had been missing Naveen, and it was evident that Naveen missed her as well, judging by how excited he had been about her hanging around his house. She didn't want to overthink any of it right now. What she needed at the moment was sleep. So, she pulled the duvet over her, stretched, and yawned before satisfactorily smiling and going to sleep.

She woke up the next morning and, making it downstairs, saw Naveen already dressed, looking like he was going to play some sort of sport. *Does he really wake up so early? And speaking of sports, what a boring lifestyle these rich men can live*, she thought to herself as she rolled her eyes and made her way toward him. He was probably going to play golf, she guessed.

Her guess was correct; he carried a bag with golf clubs and had lain them against the dining chair as he took a seat. "Boring," she said to herself.

"Good morning Sophia," he said cheerfully. "Come have breakfast with me. I hope you slept well!"

"Hum, yes, thanks. Good morning," she replied, pretending to seem unamused. She took a seat. Breakfast looked amazing, and it smelled even better. It made her feel great, even this early in the morning. Who doesn't love a nice hot meal? What better way to wake up? She tried to contain her smile and took a seat.

She looked up and caught Nikolai smiling from the kitchen doorway. "Good morning, Nikolai," she said, smiling back at him. He nodded slowly and grinned before turning away.

"How do you like my housekeeper?" Naveen asked.

"He is nice, very nice. And furthermore, he seems to cook quite well. This breakfast looks amazing!" she replied, with her mouth already half-full as she was reaching for another pancake.

"That he does," Naveen added as he was dabbing his mouth with a serviette. He stood up and placed a key beside her plate. "My car is in the garage. Nikolai can take you to it. I will be back later, so feel free to go wherever you like and make yourself at home. Nikolai will take care of anything you need." He went around to her side and played with a handful of her hair. "Please, Sophia, don't think of running away. Just be here when I come back," he whispered into her ear as he bent, placing a kiss on her temple before making his way out.

She leaned back into her chair, as her plans just might have about grown wings and flown out of the window. He had asked so lovingly, how could she even think of running away? She stood up from the table, grabbed the key, and went back upstairs.

She dressed in a pale pink loose-fitting blouse and black jeans. She decided she could at least go sightseeing, now that she wouldn't run away. She stepped out of her room and saw Nikolai passing by with laundry.

"Great, you were just the one I was looking for. Could you please show me where the garage is?" she asked politely.

"Definitely. Let me drop this, and I'll be right back," he replied.

"Sure." She rocked back on her heels and waited. The house was bigger than she thought. It had a garden and a stable as well.

"Horses!" she said in excitement. She ran ahead of Nikolai and went toward the stable. She stroked the mane of the ginger-colored horse as well as the second stallion, a white one.

"Hey, Nikolai! Do they have any names?" she called out.

He quickened his pace and reached her. "Yes, Thunder and Lightning," he said, with amusement written all over his face.

Sophia gave a spurt of laughter. "What? Thunder and Lightning?" she asked, seeming very amused.

"Yes."

"Why those names? Who's Thunder, and who's Lightning?"

"The white one is Lightning because she is fast. The other one is Thunder, as he has thunderous hooves. We had a black steed, but he died last year."

"Aww, what was his name?"

"Rocket," he said simply. She laughed again. This reminded him of how different Sophia was from Drizella. She was free-spirited, friendly, and laughed easily. She was everything Drizella wasn't but should have been. She didn't go all yuck and gross, scrunching up her nose at the horses. She didn't complain about the color of the house being too dull, and she acknowledged Nikolai's cooking, which he appreciated a lot.

The contrast was sharp and wide between the two women, and he hoped that Sophia had come to stay in Naveen's life this time around. If anyone deserved a second chance at happiness, it was his boss. He only hoped Drizella wouldn't create any problems upon learning about his boss's new relationship; the devil had a younger sister, and her name was Drizella.

Nicholai looked at Sophia and thought to himself, *Stay with him, Sophia. He needs you. He really does.*

Rick picked his phone from his desk and dialed Naveen's number, drumming his fingers on the table while waiting for the call to go through.

"Hello?" came a voice.

Rick stood up from his chair. "Naveen! When were you going to call me? I thought your plane went down the ocean or something."

"Give me a break, Rick. I did call you, but you didn't pick up the phone. Where were you then?"

Rubbing his head, Rick finally remembered he had received a late call. "Oh, yes, you did call me, but I was half asleep at the time; sorry about that! We are a few hours ahead, remember? How was your flight?" he finally asked.

"Long," Naveen replied.

"Typical. You flew first class?"

"You know I never do."

"You know you can afford it," replied Rick and laughed.

"I don't squander money; I find upgrading to first class is excessive. There are people and things I prefer to lavish my money on. You know me, Rick." Naveen said with a gentle smile.

"Yes, I do know you. I just thought that you might reconsider this time around. So, how is it going? Did you see her?" he asked.

"See who?" replied Naveen, pretending to be clueless.

"Sophia!" Rick said, smiling as if he already knew.

"How did you know she would be here?" Naveen asked, his tone laced with suspicion.

"I dropped by at her friend's coffee shop and asked about her. You must have been very tickled," said Rick as he laughed.

"I didn't know she was on the plane until I saw her boarding a taxi. Then I asked my driver to follow her. Her taxi burst a tire, so I offered her a lift, and now she's at my place." Naveen explained.

"Snoop," Rick said with a laugh.

"I didn't snoop; luck was simply on my side."

"You like her that much, huh?" asked Rick, switching to a relatively serious tone.

"Not only do I like her, but I also love her! So much that you'll be my best man again," said Naveen in an excited and hopeful voice.

"Good luck with that. And do have a swell time! Don't hurry back; spend all the time you want," said Rick, feeling happy for Naveen.

"I will do just that," replied Naveen, in a calm and relieved voice.

"I have to go; we'll talk later," Rick said before dropping the call. He sighed and shook his head. "I hope you win this time, Naveen," he whispered to himself as he hung up.

Naveen was almost back home, driving his car toward the garage. He noticed that the other car was uncovered and figured Sophia had gone out with it. He was happy she had not run away like she said she would be doing earlier on. He stepped into the house and saw Nikolai coming toward him.

"Welcome, Sir," he said, taking his bag.

"Thanks. Is Sophia in?" Naveen asked immediately.

"She stepped out a few minutes ago; she said she wanted to explore the surroundings," replied Nikolai.

"Oh, alright. Did she have any complaints or anything?" Naveen asked inquisitively.

"No, she was fine. She is very nice, and she likes horses as well."

Naveen gave him a strange look; he knew what Nikolai was implying.

"Should I serve your lunch?" asked Nikolai.

"No, not yet. Let me go and look for her; I'll be back. Take this upstairs for me, please," Naveen replied.

Naveen then handed Nikolai his jacket, and with four strides, he was out of the door, in a hurry to find Sophia. He found her at the flower bushes near the cottage, behind the main house. Hearing him approaching, she turned around. Dressed quite casually, she had never looked more beautiful to him.

"Hi," he said, not knowing how to start the conversation. He cleared his throat and tried again. "Nikolai told me you were here."

"Yes. Did you just come back?" she asked, stepping onto the sidewalk of the cottage. He took a step closer, and she froze as she felt he was getting a little too close.

"Not too long ago, just now."

He moved closer until she backed away and reached the wall of the cottage. He placed both hands at either side against the wall, leaned in, and looked right into her eyes. "You look beautiful," he then told her.

She said nothing, but she could hear her heart pounding.

"Why have you been avoiding me?" he finally asked. As he bent his face closer to hers, she could feel his warm breath against her face. Panic was building within her, to the point where she started struggling with whether to leave or stay and what to say and not to say.

"I wasn't," did she reply, trying to recover her voice, which had died down a bit.

"But you were!" Naveen brushed his lips against her nose; it felt cold. "You're scared," he added as he heard Sophia take a deep breath and bite her lip out of nervousness, turning her face away.

"I am not!" She continued arguing. He brought his left hand to cup her face and rubbed his thumb against her skin.

"If you're not, why don't you meet my gaze?" His voice was seductively alluring. He was teasing her, and he would keep doing that until she willingly gave in. He was that patient. "Look into my eyes, Sophia." He tilted her chin upward.

She saw his eyes, the mesmerizing colors that drew her like a mermaid's song would draw a sailor. "I am not scared," she said again, her voice a little louder than a whisper.

He brought his mouth close to her ear, his hair tickling her temple. He drew a line of kisses from her ear to her neck, nibbling a little with his lips as he felt the goosebumps on her skin.

"Your mask is strong, but your eyes betray you. I can see it in the way you look at me or try not to look at me," he said as he nibbled the lobe of her ear.

"See what?" Her voice was officially deserting her.

"That you want me as much as I want you," he whispered in her ear as he put his arms around her.

"That's not true."

Her arguments were useless, she knew that, but she tried anyway. She was whispering, and that alone gave her away.

"Prove me wrong," Naveen said. He then covered her mouth with his to see how she'd react to it. Whether she was willing to or not to let him kiss her, she let him, as he leaned deeper, kissing her with all the hunger he'd been feeling all this time. Seconds later, her hands were in his hair, and she finally threw her arms around him as she drew him closer.

He broke away, and she leaned back against the wall, squeezing her eyes shut and kissing him back with all her heart bursting with passion. Pinocchio syndrome or not, she had no more defenses; she let her guard down and gave in to all her desires. At this point, she couldn't remember why she'd been avoiding him all this time. It was evident she'd been missing him like crazy.

"I was right, wasn't I?" he asked, kissing her lightly. "Say it, say you want me, Sophia Bill. Say it!" He demanded softly but firmly.

"Yes! Yes, I do want you," she said as she breathed onto his skin and held him tighter, looking into his eyes. "I want you inside of me. I want you to make love to me. I want to feel you deep inside of me, to kiss me until I am breathless. I want to hear you say my name over and over again. It's like music to my ears. Yes, Naveen. I do want you." She poured her heart out as she could feel her face turn beet red.

He smiled victoriously. As he kissed her and carried her, she wrapped her legs around his waist.

"I needed to hear it from you," he said. He went through the back door of the cottage; he was sure it would be open. He shut it behind him with his foot as they came in enlaced.

Chapter Four

The week went by very fast, almost in a blur. The house had a livelier aura with Sophia around, which made Nikolai smile more often; it was like all seasons had come at once, with the sun shining over the house all day, all week, all year. He knew that whatever went on between Sophia and his boss was none of his business, but that made him smile to himself anyway. His boss was happy, the way he had never been since he had married the witch dressed in women's skin and fancy clothing.

Sophia was good at gardening and with colors, so Nikolai had asked her opinion as to which flowers to keep and which ones to abandon in the house. She always had a puzzled and uncertain look on her face; despite that, she would tell him what she thought, and most times, it would work. The house had come to appear more like a home than a bachelor's mansion, much to Naveen's pleasure.

Since Sophia had to be leaving soon, the house had gone relatively silent. Naveen had come to believe that her laughter caused the flowers to bloom and that the sky would definitely turn gray in her absence. He did not like it, for he had developed an affinity for the sun shining on him all the time. He finally understood why people called it feeling blue. No bright color could define the feeling he was going through at this moment.

The debate in his head was no match for the one that went on upstairs.

"Do you really have to leave?" he asked as he watched her fold her clothes, forming a neat pile on the bed.

She was rolling her eyes. "That's the sixteenth time you've asked me, Naveen."

"That's because I don't want you to leave," he replied, putting his arms around her lower stomach from behind and resting his chin on her soft shoulder. "Please stay a little longer. I don't think I am ready for the goodbyes yet." He made her turn around so she could face him. "My flight is in two days; we could leave together then."

"You know I have to go now," she said, snaking her arms around his neck. She smelled like home; she felt like home in his embrace.

"We could book you on another flight."

He smiled brightly, marveling at his own idea.

"Really, Naveen?"

She laughed once, and then her expression turned serene again. "It's still morning, and I'll be here all afternoon," she told him, giving him a lingering, soft kiss on his cheek. The warm sensation of her lips remained on his skin long after she had parted.

"It somehow doesn't make it any better," he said grumpily. "I want you here with me all day," he added as he snuggled his face into her neck and breathed the banana strawberry scent of her shampoo. "Right here. Always," he said again.

"I have to go, Naveen."

"Hmm. Guess we still have a few hours then." He expressed quietly, with his hand slowly roaming across her back until he found her zipper. "How about now? Do you still wish to leave?" His eyes shone as he devoured her appearance like an animal waiting to be fed after going hungry for several days.

"Naveen," she whispered breathily, almost inaudibly. He had his way of sending her voice away. He could gladly quiet her like this forever.

"For me," he replied, as her dress slid off her delicate shoulders, down her thin waist, ending at the bottom of her feet. "I want to remember every moment of Vienna. With you. Right here with me."

"But Nikolai—"

"He won't bother us."

And he didn't, as they savored each moment as if their life depended on it.

Sophia called Naveen as soon as she got home, but he was not around, as Nikolai answered. She laughed when Nikolai mentioned how much everyone and everything missed her.

"Even the boss has grown gray hair thinking about you," he added. He mentioned keeping the house shipshape till she returned. "I'll plant tulips as well. Do call more often, will you?" he said, in such a manner that she could sense his beaming smile at the other end.

"Yes, I will, Nikolai. I hope to see you again."

"Certainly!" he said excitedly, with unwavering confidence.

She looked around her room after the call had ended. It looked the same and felt very strange. She missed Vienna and the way she didn't have to worry about so many things while she was away. But here she was again, face to face with the responsibilities she had left behind. There was a knock on the door.

"May I come in?" It was her sister.

She stood up to open the door. "Julie? You're back?"

"Yes, I am. I've been around since the second day you left. Mom told me you went on a vacation."

"Yes, I went to Vienna; I really needed a break," she said as they both sat on the bed. "So, tell me, how is college?"

"Not you too! Why does everyone keep asking me these boring questions? College is on fire." Julie pouted slightly.

Sophia gasped, taking it literally. "Your college is on fire?"

"No, silly. I mean, it's exciting. You know how it is; you've been there as well. So, tell me about you, how's your boutique? I saw that Corinne has a new coffee shop; her lattes are the bomb. How was the vacation? Where did you go? Whom did you meet? Tell me everything!" Julie rolled excitedly, seeming almost too animated but in an endearing way.

"Easy there, easy. We have all day to talk about it. I'll tell you everything one after the other," Sophia said with a grin.

"You have a point. Mom says you haven't found a husband yet." She smiled impishly.

"What kind of a question is that? Give me a break! Did you come home with one?"

"No, I—"

"So there! Don't pester me, sister." Sophia threw a pillow at her sister playfully.

"I've got my eyes on you, sis," Julie replied, widening her eyes dramatically.

"Stop talking rubbish."

"Anyway, come downstairs for dinner; Mom made pot roast. And Dad, he tells the best jokes," she said as she stood up.

"Dad?" Sophia looked confused for a moment, and then it seemed to hit her. "Oh, him," she added, biting her lip.

"Yes, him." There was a brief silence. "Sophia, you still haven't accepted him, have you?" Julie sighed and placed a hand on Sophia's shoulder. "We're so different, you know, you and me—complete opposites. I'm lousier than you are, zesty and sassy with my forwardness. I'm everywhere all at once! But you...no, you're more reserved, you have a bigger heart, and you've always been more particular about everyone's happiness."

Sophia stared at her sister, wondering where she was going.

"You're selfless, loving, hardworking, and beautiful, and sometimes, sometimes, I envy you." Julie's voice was filled with awe and a lot of adoration.

"Julie—"

"I'm not finished," she added, raising her index finger. "You were the one who was able to get through to me when the crippling depression got the better out of me after Dad's death. You helped Mom smile again, and you made us realize that if he were here, he would also want us to move on and be happy. So, why are you the one stuck in the past now? Mom finally decided to be happy, but you are another reason she's sad."

Julie sucked in a breath and sat down to face her sister. "Selfish, isn't it, Sophia? When you are happy, everyone is happy. Mom is happy, I am happy, and even Dad...even Dad is happy. And I mean, I know you get that." Sophia looked at her sister with a frown; it was obvious she didn't like the discussion.

"Accepting that man downstairs, whom our mom loves so much and wants to start a new life with, would mean the world to her. I mean, haven't you seen the glow on her face whenever they are together? The last time her face glowed this much was when our father was alive. Would you be selfish enough to let that glow fade away just because you don't like him? If you don't like him, then fine, don't accept him. You'll be responsible for her sadness and mine because I hate to see her unhappy. And if you're doing this for Dad, he wouldn't be happy either." Julie crossed her arms as she stared out of the window.

"Julie—"

"No, Sophia. I won't let you argue your way out of this again, not today." Julie wiped the tears on her face and stood up. "Come down for dinner, please, for everyone's sake. Give him a chance and get to know him. I promise you'll see why Mother loves him so much."

Sophia locked the door after her sister left. She could feel her stubbornness begin to wane. She pulled out a photo from her bedside drawer and became immersed in thought. *Dad, have I really made you unhappy? Have my actions been making you sad? I got so carried away with my anger that I didn't realize my actions were hurting everybody I love. I am so stubborn. I'm sorry, I'm so sorry. But I'll make it all better, I'll fix my mistakes, and I will make everybody happy again.*

Her phone rang as she stood up. She answered it with, "Hey, Corinne."

"Hey, girl," Corinne said, the excitement in her voice fizzling like a soft drink. "Wait, have you been crying?"

"No...yes...I mean no, okay, maybe a little." Sophia admitted, smiling at Corinne's ability to detect her sadness from two words spoken over the phone.

"Really, now! You just got back, and you're crying? What's the matter?" Corinne sounded concerned, even pensive now.

"We'll talk later."

"Alright. Take care." Corinne understood that perhaps Sophia needed some time for herself.

Sophia stopped at the bottom of the stairs, noticing how her family's laughter rang through the house as her mother served the food. She looked from person to person and realized she had been missing out on a lot. She felt guilty again.

George looked up from the table. "Sophia?" Everyone else looked up, too. Cleo, her mother, dropped the napkin and came to her.

"What is the matter, sweetie? Why do you look so sad?"

"I'm sorry, Mom, I've been very foolish. I didn't realize I had been hurting you…." Sophia's voice sounded heavier and teary.

"Please, don't say anymore." Cloe covered her lips with her hand, her eyes welling up too.

"I'm sorry," Sophia repeated her apologies to her mother. Then, she moved over to the other side of the table and looked at George right in the eyes. "I am so sorry for how I have acted with you, George."

"Sophia," George started, "I am not offended by your actions. I was hoping this moment would come, and it has, and I am so glad, really glad. I love your mother, Sophia, and I can give you my word that this will never change. I will love you and your sister as my own daughters if you allow me."

Sophia nodded, unable to talk, emotions flooding her system like waves settling in after a storm.

Julie sighed in relief and embraced her sister. "Ha, I love happy endings. We should take a picture to capture this moment! Everyone is so emotional. Come on, Mom, don't make me cry as well! Be happy; you have every right to be. Say cheese!" Julie sniffed.

"There's no camera," Cleo said, laughing.

"It's a virtual camera," Julie replied with a wink. "Group hug!" she said as she wrapped her arms around her family.

Everything felt better, like gray clouds retreating to reveal a magnificent sun. Everything was going to be alright. Sophia would live life, one day at a time, with her family – her complete family.

Chapter Five

Four Weeks Later.

Bella drove into the premises and spotted her husband, who was talking to a few people outside the building. She honked to draw his attention, and he looked up. Frowning in confusion, he excused himself and strode toward the car, wondering what might be up with her.

"Hi there," she said, smiling brightly.

"Aren't you supposed to be resting?" he asked as he opened the door to sit in the front seat. He then leaned and kissed her lightly. "What are you doing here?"

"I got bored of staying at home. I went to the salon and did some grocery shopping. How do you like my hair?" asked Bella, as she batted her eyelashes, to which he grinned.

"It's beautiful! I like the tresses. But really, you should be resting." He frowned slightly once again.

"I was bored, Rick, but I am perfectly fine now. I have been around the city and have not collapsed, not even once. Listen, why don't we have lunch together?"

"That's a good idea; give me a minute. I'll be right back." He looked back again and asked before stepping out, "Are you sure you are fine?" His tone was still a bit hesitant.

"Rick, I'm fine, hurry on now," she replied, pushing him slightly.

"I believe you," he said, after a little contemplation, and then laughed as he opened the door to get out.

Julie barged into the coffee shop, sending scared looks flying in her direction. She seemed oblivious of the reaction she had caused as she headed straight for the counter. "Where's Corinne?" she asked, sounding out of breath.

"She's in there," Leela answered, pointing toward the inner door.

"Corinne!" Julie shouted, opening the door with a bang, while Leela wondered what was wrong with her; she was no different from a thunderstorm. Restless and wild.

"What is the matter with you? Why do you look so scared? Is everything okay?" Corinne asked.

"I can't find Sophia!" Julie's voice was high-pitched and shook.

Corinne looked lost, and as it sank in, she started shaking her head and went on. "What do you mean you can't find Sophia? Don't be overdramatic. She should be at the boutique right now."

"No! She isn't. She was supposed to be there, true, but she isn't there, and she isn't here either." Julie was beginning to wheeze now.

"Julie, have a seat and breathe. Come on, breathe; there, slowly, calmly, breathe." Corrine tried to wrap her head around the situation while she attempted to calm Julie down. "There, there, good, just stay calm and remember to breathe; I'll try to call her."

"Her phone is switched off." Julie sounded as if someone had hit her in the toe with a hammer.

"I said breathe. Switched off? Perhaps her battery died...." Corrine wasn't sure if she was telling this to Julie or herself.

"No! You don't understand! Her car...her car was found halfway to the boutique; the door was left open. Oh dear, I wonder what has happened to her!" Julie cried, covering her face with her hands. Her body was shaking slightly.

"Julie, breathe, just breathe, she will be fine. We are going to find her. Do you hear me, Julie? We'll find Sophia." Julie repeatedly nodded, finding it very hard to stay calm.

"Have you spoken to Naveen?"

"No, I happen not to have his phone number, so I didn't think about it. I just came running here after calling Mom to let her know about this. Oh, dear, I wonder where she might be. You see, even her keys were still in the car, which is not good."

"I'll call him right away; this doesn't sound good indeed." But before Corrine could reach out to him, her phone rang; it was Naveen.

"Hello, Corinne, have you seen Sophia?" Naveen blurted out as soon as she answered the call.

"No, I was about to call you to ask you the same thing," she said frantically.

"We found her car on the way to her boutique; the door left open with the keys still in the ignition. Somehow, for some reason, someone might have taken her. I've called the police to file a missing person report, and they're on it already, as circumstances are very strange." Naveen rolled out the information.

"Alright, thank you for letting me know. And please, do not hesitate calling me if you need anything."

"Who was that?" Julie asked, standing up.

"Naveen. He found her car. He said he's called the police. Who do you think might have taken her, and if that's the case, why?"

"I don't know, but they better not harm my sister." Julie tried to gulp the lump in her throat, her eyes watering as she tried.

"Let's hope she is fine. Come on; we should go to the police station," Corinne said, rubbing her arm.

"Yes."

"Leela!" Corrine shouted out as they got out of the office.

"Don't worry; I'll take care of everything here. Go, and make sure we find her," Leela replied, with a serene look on her face.

"Thanks, Leela," Corrine said as she took Julie's hand and stepped out.

The police had not found any leading clues, but it was declared a kidnapping case. "The question is, who would want to kidnap her?" the officer in charge of the investigation asked them all this same question several times, but unfortunately, none of them had an answer. Julie looked like she would pass out at any moment, while Naveen didn't look any better. Rick had arrived with his wife; he had gotten the news just as they were leaving the restaurant where they had had lunch. Corinne had gone home with Cleo when realizing that Sophia's mother couldn't handle the shock that her daughter had been kidnapped. The atmosphere reeked of panic, and they all jumped when Naveen's cell phone suddenly rang.

The voice on the other end startled him. "Hello there, Naveen."

"Drizella?" His face was changing color with anger. He wanted to go out to continue the call, but he somehow decided against it.

"I'm sure you must be wondering why I'm calling you out of the blue. After all, I haven't called you in weeks," she drawled. "I've been watching you, Naveen. I told you, I will make you pay for what you did to me."

"I have done you no harm, Drizella," Naveen said, trying his best to remain calm.

"I wouldn't be so sure about that if I were you!" She snapped back. Her voice had an icy edge to it, which gave him a very bad feeling.

"Why are you calling me?" he asked, gritting his teeth.

"I have news that might interest you. A five-foot, seven inches tall brunette who also owns Mega glamour boutique. Does that ring a bell?"

"What do you know about her disappearance?" he asked, putting the phone on speaker. His heart was beating wildly.

"Well, let's just say I know a little too much, like where she is and who took her. I could tell you who took her, but certainly not where she is." She teased.

"Where is she, Drizella?" It was taking Naveen all his might to keep his cool.

"Aren't your ears working properly? I said I'll tell you who, not where. So that you know, I do have your girl pet with me...."

"If you as much as lay a finger on her, Drizella, I'll...." Naveen's breathing turned erratic.

"Empty threats," she scoffed. "You can't find me, and if you can't find me, you can't find her."

"Driz—"

"Cheerio!" she said before ending the call.

"This lunatic of a woman," he growled in anger, staring down at his phone as if he could see her through the phone.

"We may be able to trace the call," Rick said hurriedly. "It was long enough. We can trace where she was speaking from and then find out where she is. That's her Achilles' heel."

"You're right," the officer said before setting out to work.

Moments later, they had the location. "It's a deserted road," Rick said. "I know where it is. It's not used so much, which is an advantage for her because no one will think of that place."

"It's not an advantage," Naveen said, his voice now having a deadly calmness. "It's the biggest mistake of her life. The last one she will ever make. Let's go."

"I want to go with you." Julie offered.

"No, Julie, you can't; it's too dangerous. Go home with Bella and give your mom updates. We'll be back as soon as we can," Rick said.

"But—"

"He's right, Julie. Drizella is a crooked woman; she can do anything. Go home, and don't stop praying. Come on, officer," Naveen added. Rick and Naveen, in their desire to assist in saving Sophia, just seemed to be taking over the officer's role.

They branched at Naveen's house to see whether they could find something to track Drizella down. "Something that has her scent on it, as we will need to use dogs in case she escapes," said the officer. They found a shawl. It was one of the few things she had forgotten to take with her when she packed her things and left his house.

"How much longer before we get there?" Naveen asked, running his fingers in his hair. He was shifting in his seat, looking extremely nervous.

"Relax, Naveen; we're almost there. Just a few meters ahead according to these coordinates. And if I'm right, it should be that building over there," Rick said, stopping the car a few meters away and pointing to what looked like a deserted building.

"It's an old warehouse," the officer said while pressing his walkie-talkie button. "We have found the location. I repeat, we have found the location."

Criminals are so cliché, Naveen thought, rolling his eyes. "Please tell the others not to come blasting their sirens; we need to attract little or no attention."

"Affirmative."

The warehouse was empty and extremely dirty; it was obvious it hadn't been used in years.

"I don't get it," Rick said, looking puzzled. "The GPS said right here, but there's no one here."

"These people are not so smart, sir. Look, footmarks," the officer said as he looked at the dirty floor. There were footprints in the dust, and they obviously belonged to none of them. "They must be around here unless they have left already."

"No, they couldn't have left; the signal is quite strong, they're...." The officer saw Naveen put his ear to the ground. "What in blazes are you doing?"

Naveen motioned for everyone to keep quiet, as several other police officers were just arriving.

"I think this place has a basement; I can hear voices." The side of his face had picked up dust, but he didn't seem to care. "We have to find the entrance."

The warehouse was just one big room. There were no adjoining parts to the building, except for the door that led to the back, and it was locked from the inside. Rick tripped over something and fell, but an officer caught him before he hit the ground.

"I tripped on something." He turned to take a look at the floor. It was a door handle. They had found the way to the basement.

For the past 30 hours, Drizella had kept Sophia trapped against her will, and even though she had not planned it that way initially, she was ready not to let her go soon. She was jealous of Sophia. Not because Sophia was so beautiful; Drizella was herself very attractive. But Sophia had one thing that Drizella would give her life for; she had Naveen's heart.

Drizella felt her blood had turned into poison, seeing how Naveen was going crazy caring for Sophia. Sophia had her eyes on him, and Drizella could see how desperate he now was to find her safe and sound. This pushed Drizella on edge; she started being cruel to Sophia.

Sophia was scared at first but somehow knew that Drizella would never hurt her physically. She had this feeling that Drizella had this plan of only hurting her emotionally. She could feel that Drizella would soon start intimidating her and say anything simply to diminish her.

And this is exactly what Drizella did. She started name-calling Sophia. She used yelling and screaming, menacing to harm Sophia's friends and family members. And she went as far as threatening to commit suicide.

During this whole session of emotional torture, as Sophia was trying to wriggle under the tight bindings of the rope restraining her, Drizella accidentally kicked her. The chair that Sophia was sitting on rolled to one side, with Sophia's face hitting the chair's handle while falling hard on the floor; she was left with a number of bruises.

"You cannot snatch him from me," Sophia said. "I will never let you. Naveen is and will always be mine only."

Drizella kept on playing her mental cruelty scenario, but at this point, Sophia's mind stopped working completely. She was in a state of shock and trauma but somehow managed to let it slip out of her mouth, "He can never love you again, Drizella. Not after this."

Drizella's face turned purple after hearing this, which made her realize that something had gone seriously wrong with her behavior. Too panicked to even think about her next step, she was taken by surprise by the police and Naveen.

God! I should have known they were going to track my phone call. How could I have been so careless? Drizella thought. She heard a growl behind her; two dogs were coming after her, barking, as she tried to think of a way to escape. Within moments, the whole place was being surrounded. This was when she pointed a gun at one of the officers as they were closing in on her.

"Stop! Stop right there, or I shoot!" she shouted. She looked at the officer's name tag. "Stop right there, Ryan."

"Drop your weapon; you are totally outnumbered," Officer Ryan said.

"I said, stop!" she replied. But the gun went off accidentally. The attack was swift; none of them saw it coming. She had fired into the air as one of the dogs lunged at her arm. Shrieking in terror, she dropped her gun.

"We will need paramedics; someone call an ambulance!" One of the policemen looked up to see who this was coming from. It was Naveen, holding Sophia in his arms. She was semi-unconscious, and her face was black and blue. She looked dangerously pale while Naveen was becoming even paler. In fact, he seemed to be on the verge of throwing up or fainting. He was so absorbed in helping Sophia that he did not even think of looking at Drizella.

Officer Ryan approached Drizella as she was holding her bleeding arm, her face contorted in pain. "You have a lot of questions to answer, Madam. You are under arrest."

As the ambulance arrived, Naveen looked like he was ready to jump on Drizella. "You!" he growled. "You dare to touch her again! I wish that dog had ripped off your face. You're nothing but a demon! I will make you suffer; you will spend a very long time in jail. That, I can promise you." At this point, Naveen had a fire burning in his eyes.

"Let's go, Naveen; the ambulance is here," Rick said, tugging at Naveen's shirt.

"I will…." Naveen's eyes were boring into Drizella.

"Let's go, Naveen!" Rick nudged at Naveen's arm, and they left.

Naveen was pacing up and down the hospital corridor. Cleo sat there with a distant look on her face. She had cried so much that her face was red and swollen, like a tomato.

"Julie, that's the fifth cocoa you're drinking." Corinne pointed out. "Sophia will be fine."

"I can't stay calm, and I keep feeling thirsty," she said in exasperation.

"You'll become bloated at this rate. Come here, sit beside me. Come." Corinne patted the chair beside her.

Julie looked at her and asked, "How do you get to be so strong? I would probably spend a zillion years trying to figure it out."

Corinne shrugged. "It won't look so good if all of us are crying our eyes out now, will it? I know Sophia will be alright; I just know it."

The doctor came out of the room. "Mr. Hawk?" he asked.

Naveen's head shot up. "How is she? Is she going to be alright?" His eyes were red. Julie wondered if he had secretly been crying.

"She will be fine," was what the doctor started with. He then continued, "She is mainly suffering from a minor head injury, a concussion to be more precise, probably caused by a fall. This occurs when the impact on the head is severe enough to cause brain injury. It is thought to be the result of the brain hitting against the hard walls of your skull or the forces of sudden acceleration and deceleration. As it is a closed head injury, there is no break of the skull. With minor head injuries like these, there are no symptoms other than pain at the site of the injury. As it is, she should be taking acetaminophen to fight the pain and simply rest."

Although none of them said anything, they had all started feeling a little relieved.

Naveen sighed and leaned his head back on the headrest of the bench that he was sitting on. With her signature smile, Sophia sneaked into his memories. He remembered how he first met her. It was still fresh in his mind as if it had happened yesterday. It was a bright morning amidst the fall. Dried orange leaves were loitering around, looking strangely beautiful. Naveen was sitting alone, enjoying the silence and a latte when his eyes lingered to a beautiful face through the glass window of the café, and the time suddenly went still. It was as if all four seasons had come at once; it was raining while the sun blazed, with the snowmen roaming around the streets chasing the orange leaves.

The girl was laughing while playing with a stray dog, unbothered by people passing by. She had no idea that she was making a man fall in love with her, ready to give away all that he possessed, with all his heartbeats and might. Naveen was a very practical man who had never believed in love at first sight. This girl, though, changed his perceptions about a lot of things, including love, just by existing, just by suddenly appearing.

Naveen wished he could go pet the dog with her and tuck her hair behind her head. The dark curls that seemed to trouble her as the wind ruffled them each time it passed; they seemed to have an urge to kiss her. The dog licked her hands and then her face, making her laugh even harder. She suddenly fell back and slightly rubbed her butt as she continued to laugh. That stranger had stirred some long-lost emotions within Naveen, and for an instant, he had felt jealous of the dog. He had laughed about it later; how could he feel jealous of a dog? That was crazy, but he guessed it had to be love.

The waitress called him and asked if he needed something, which brought him out of his ecstasy.

"Hunh?" Naveen was raising his brows at the hostess.

"I was asking if you needed anything else?" She was batting her eyelashes at him.

"No, no. I am good. Thank you," Naveen had replied while instantly looking out of the window again. His heart had sunk in the pits of his stomach; the girl was gone. The dog sat there beside the road, looking sad and lost. Naveen threw money on the table and left the café.

"Hey, you. Sad, aren't you?" He had walked to the dog, who had started wagging its tail at him. "Do you know her? The girl?" Naveen asked the dog as if it could speak. "Yeah, I know. She is beautiful, but where did she go?" He looked around, his eyes scanning everyone on the street, trying to find that one specific face, but she was not there.

He had then felt empty and lost, as if he was all alone on the planet while Earth's oxygen was slowly running out. Today, sitting on a cold plastic bench in the hospital, Naveen was feeling the same emptiness, but this time it was more intense. He closed his eyes and prayed harder than he had ever done before. "Please, bring her

back, please!" He begged, but his own voice echoed inside

his empty heart. A tear rolled down his cheek and got lost

inside his collar. "You will pay for it, Drizella. I promise

you."

Chapter Six

It had been three weeks since Sophia's dramatic incident. Although she was doing a lot better and seemed like she was getting back to her normal self, she kept more to herself and away from everyone. She assured her mom everything was fine, but her attitude made everyone justifiably worried. It was as if she had contained herself inside her body.

"I wonder what is wrong with her," George said at breakfast one morning. "She's so lost in her thought process these days, hardly talks to anybody. It is getting me worried." Cleo sighed, staring at him.

"I've been trying to talk to her, but she keeps saying everything is fine. Would you try to chat with her, Julie?" Cleo asked.

"She's not telling me anything either, and Naveen says she has not been answering his calls," Julie replied with a frown.

"I'm really scared. Do you think she hasn't gotten over the incident yet?" Cleo said, her face visibly etched with worry.

"I think it's something else." Julie mused.

"Is her boutique not doing very well?" asked George now.

"She hasn't even been there in about four days now." Julie was chewing on a granola bar, looking lost.

"I'm worried something is wrong with her," Cleo said.

"I'm fine," Sophia said, coming down the stairs. Her face was pale, and she had left her hair loose, which framed her pretty face like a curtain.

"Aren't you going to eat breakfast?" her mom asked.

"No, I'll eat later. I'm going to work." She was walking toward the door.

"Sophia…." Cleo called out. Too late, she was already out of the house.

There was a prolonged silence and then a sigh.

"Something's certainly wrong. She is behaving really strange now." Julie burst out.

"I agree." George nodded. "And we have to find out what it is."

"Hey, have you by any chance seen Sophia today?" Naveen was asking Corinne.

"No, I haven't," she said, taking out mugs from a shelf and setting them on the table. "Have you?"

"I wouldn't be asking you if I had. Oddly, I've been calling her for days, and she's not picking up or returning my messages. Am I the only one who thinks she's acting strange?" Naveen was chewing on his lip, looking at his feet.

"Nope, everyone does. Her mom is worried sick, thinking about her." Corinne kept the mugs on the counter and rubbed her palms together. "She is not our Sophia these days," she said, putting her hands in her pockets.

"If you see her, tell her to please pick my calls." Naveen pleaded.

"Hold up, lover boy; she's not picking mine either. It's like she's avoiding everybody. Maybe she grew goblin ears, and she wants no one to see them." Corinne shrugged and grinned.

"Very funny," Naveen replied drily.

"Yes, I know it's a bad joke and very bad timings, but I don't know what is going on. I'm also as clueless as you are."

"Perhaps we should pay her a visit tonight." Naveen suggested.

"Tonight?" Corinne tilted her head sideways, rolling her tongue in her cheek. "That's a good idea, but I've got tonight fixed. How about tomorrow?"

"Sounds like forever," he grumbled. Corinne rolled her eyes.

"I know Sophia; she'll talk when she gets bored of keeping to herself. I am worried too, really. We'll see her tomorrow. Tonight is sardine-packed for me; the thought of it is making my head spin already."

"Alright. Tomorrow it is," he said as he stood up. "I'll come pick you up."

"No problem." She watched him leave and then sighed deeply; her head was beginning to throb. Two sleepless nights in a row, one more tonight, and she was sure she would collapse. "Leela." She hesitated a bit. "I need a bit of a favor from you."

"Hey, you don't have to be so formal with me. You need to rest; I can see that. You have bags under your eyes, and even your boisterous attitude is waning. I can't have you collapse on me. Come on, take the rest of the day off. As long as I'm here, you have nothing to worry about."

Corinne drew her assistant in a bear hug. "Thanks so much, Leela. I don't know what I'd do without you. Thank you!"

Sophia made sure they were all asleep before she left; she thought it was best for everyone. She would go far away so they wouldn't see her sorrows or her dilemma. Everyone would probably get over the shock in a few months, and maybe one day, when she had enough courage to face them, she would return. But until then, she had to leave everyone and everything behind. She muffled a sob and dropped a note on the table. She had paid a taxi driver to pick her up and drop her at the closest hotel to the airport, as she knew taking her car would wake someone up. Julie and her mother were light sleepers. She took a last long look at the house as she whispered, "I'm sorry," to no one in particular.

Rick was sure he saw Sophia get into a taxi. He had gone back for something at the office and took a shorter route home, which went past Sophia's house. He thought about following the taxi but dismissed himself as being paranoid. "It's just past nine, Rick; she probably wants to go see someone," he had told himself.

The reality struck him in the face the next day when Naveen called him with the news. "Sophia is gone."

"Gone, where?" Rick sputtered over a cup of water.

"I don't know; nobody knows. She dropped a note last night filled with funny things. It said she's sorry she had to leave this way, but it was best for everyone...."

"Oh, no."

"Oh no, what? Do you know anything?"

"Naveen, I'm sorry, I should have called you last night when I saw her. She was getting into a taxi, and I thought she probably was going to see a friend, so I didn't bother following her."

"Gosh, damn it. What have you done, Rick? She only has so many friends, and if she wanted to see one of them, she could have gone in her car."

"I just didn't want to be paranoid, Naveen...."

"I get it. I...I'm not blaming you. Everyone is so tensed right now; it wouldn't be right to blame anyone."

"I'm sorry, Naveen." Rick scratched his neck and muttered apologetically.

"Stop apologizing and get over here; we need to figure out where she could be." Naveen was agitated, and so was the entire family. "Where are you, Sophia? Where are you?"

Drizella had been put up for questioning, but she refused to say anything, insisting she would only talk to

Naveen. Exasperation was all over his face when he did arrive with Rick.

"What is it? Why are you making it hard for the police to do their job?" he said through gritted teeth, his voice as harsh as a glass cutting edge.

"Whoa, hold it right there," she said. "Don't use that electricity tone on me. Face off with whoever's stepped on your tail. I just wanted to talk."

"I don't think I have anything to say to you except to go to hell!" He lashed out.

"Naveen, you need to calm down," Rick said gently.

"Make this woman understand I have nothing to discuss with her, and nothing she says will make me withdraw my charges against her. She's going to spend a long time in prison; otherwise, I would stop calling myself Naveen Hawk," he said, storming out of the interrogation room.

There was a long pause in the room, and after a while, Rick sighed. "What do you want, Drizella?" he asked while he sat on a chair. "What do you want? Money, half of what he owns, or his life?"

Drizella took a long and hard look at Rick. "I want love. I want a friend, a companion," she said quietly, as her eyes had lost some of their ferocity. "I want happiness and a home and a man to call mine. I had everything, but I lost it. I realized too late everything I had. A little too late."

"How late?"

"When I saw that his heart was no longer with me but with Sophia."

"That was after the divorce."

"Yes," she said, laughing bitterly. "She is a lucky woman."

"You were jealous."

"Very," she said, leaning forward. "You don't know how it feels watching another woman taking your place and realizing you were the one who foolishly gave it away."

Rick was silent. As Drizella talked to him, he could not begin to explain how weird the situation was.

"Why are you telling me this?" he asked cautiously.

"It makes me feel better," she said, shrugging. "I'm not as bad as you think I am, or as I appear to be with what I have done to Sophia. My problem has always been that I was never satisfied with what I had." She blinked rapidly, perhaps to push the tears back. The truth was consuming her sanity; Rick could see that. He wondered how much strength it took her to admit so much finally.

"You had problems with Naveen from the moment you guys got married."

"I did. I'm such a dumbass." She laughed bitterly. "I left him on the second day of our honeymoon. I created so many problems for him while all he ever did was trying to make me happy. I told him I wanted no babies, and he was fine with it, or at least he pretended to be. I know how much he loves children. Yet…I would deserve an award for the most discontented woman on Earth."

"He never told me any of that," Rick added, shaking his head.

"Were you expecting him to? It's a personal matter; he wouldn't tell you all this. And then, one day, he got drunk."

"At a party…." Rick said, sitting up, reining in his defense.

"And cheated on me."

"He made a mistake."

"With my friend!"

"Everyone makes mistakes, Drizella."

"But I couldn't forgive him for that."

"So, you divorced him."

"That was my mistake, and I regret it every day, every moment." She lightly punched the table.

"You didn't seem remorseful. Instead, you kept causing him more and more pain—"

"Driving him to another woman."

"Whom you abducted," Rick said with an edge of accusation.

"All I did was trying to get back at him because I felt…I felt he did me a lot of wrong with what he did, and to me, my anger was justified. But that day, with the way he reacted when he found her back, I realized he is a man who has space in his heart for just one woman, and that woman isn't me." She sniffed. "I lost. I lost everything. I'm so stupid." She sobbed almost hysterically.

Rick watched her, speechless. He had no more comments or things to say. He gave her his handkerchief from his pocket and slowly headed out of the room, but not before she could say, "Rick, tell Naveen I said I'm sorry for everything." He nodded.

"And one more thing. The truth is, I don't deserve anything. Our agreement was a right to half the property in case our marriage broke after three years, but we didn't even get to spend two together. One way or the other, do tell him I'm sorry, and I'm happy for him as well; he does deserve her." She was silent for a moment. "And also, thanks for the handkerchief."

The house was silent. It had been two days, and they still had no idea where Sophia was. They had combed every hotel in the area, but none of them had her name on their list.

"I'm going to lose my mind the way this is going," Naveen said, holding his head in his hands.

"Tell me about it," Julie replied, sinking deeper into her sofa. She sat up again, saying, "She should at least have the common sense of calling someone. How can she disappear like that? It's been two days, Mom, two days!" Her voice was high-pitched and was dripping with worry and anger at Sophia.

"Everyone is counting the days, Julie; don't make it worse," Cleo said, rubbing her back.

Julie sunk back into her couch. "She can be so silly, you know. I don't know how big of a problem she might have that she'd be so embarrassed to tell anyone about it." She sighed. "My head hurts just thinking about where she might be. It's like looking for a needle in a haystack."

"What if…" George started speculatively, "what if she were still in the city but living somewhere under another name?" There was a long silence, as it could be a possibility; they were all considering this might be happening.

"That's even worse than her being out of the country." Corinne mused, fiddling with the dining table cloth.

Naveen seemed lost in his thoughts. "I don't know why I have this hunch that she is hiding right under our nose, but George might be right."

"You mean like the house basement?" Julie said sarcastically.

"No, not that close, but somewhere…it's a hunch, a very strong one."

"I'd sooner be in Notre Dame if your hunch proved to be right." Julie teased.

"Very funny, Julie," Naveen replied.

Corinne looked at the clock on the wall. "I have to leave now…."

"Yes. Yes, I understand. Thank you so much, Corinne. My daughter is lucky she has a friend like you," Cleo said.

"No, you don't have to thank me. You guys are like family to me," she said, with a little smile, the light in her eyes flickering a little. "You are the family I never had. And if Sophia were my sister, I'd do the same for her."

"Add sweetness to the situation, and the problem doesn't look so big," Julie said, sitting up. "It would be fun to have two older sisters, though, particularly when one of them is not on a self-imposed exile."

"You know you're always welcome here, Corinne, anytime," George added.

"Thank you so much," Corinne said. "I know we will find Sophia, and it won't be long before we do."

"Well, I hope she is in better shape this time. The last time she went missing, you said we'd find her, but she wasn't looking so good in the end." Julie quipped impishly. Corinne gawked in disbelief as she looked at Cleo.

"Can you hear what she's saying to me?"

"Hey, I'm just teasing," Julie said, fleeing as Corinne was advancing toward her.

"You take that back right now."

"Okay, I'm sorry." She laughed. There was a little more lightness as everyone started laughing, the tension in the atmosphere dropping a little. Corinne's phone rang.

"Hello? Hello? I can't hear you, hello?" She was frowning in confusion and was going to end the call when she heard a sob at the other end.

"Corinne?" The voice was a little louder than a whisper.

"Who is this?" she asked, perplexed.

"It's Sophia." She sounded like she had lost her voice.

"Sophia? Girl, where are you? Everyone's worried sick about you. How could you leave without telling anyone? Where are you?"

"Corinne...."

"Are you doing alright? And your voice, what happened to your voice? You—"

"Corinne! Please, I can't answer all of these questions, not at the moment, but I promise I'm fine."

"Where are you?"

"I can't tell you right now. I want to tell you something else, but I need to be sure you're not with Naveen."

Corinne frowned. Not with Naveen? That was odd. "No." She lied. "I'm not with Naveen." She looked at him, motioning him to keep quiet. He raised his eyebrows in suspicion.

"Corinne." There was a deep sigh, and Corinne waited, not expecting what came next. "I'm pregnant."

Corinne was taken by surprise. "You're what?"

"I'm pregnant, Corinne; I'm pregnant," she said, crying over the phone.

"But how? Who? Why? Where? I mean, who's responsible?" The answer was obvious, but she took no wild guesses.

"Naveen. That's why I said I want to be sure you're not around him. I don't want him to find out."

"He's bound to find out sooner or later. Running away wasn't the best option."

Corinne heard a masculine voice in the background. "Who was that?" she asked Sophia.

"I'll talk to you later, Corinne. Bye."

"No, wait, hold on." The call ended.

"Was that Sophia? Where is she?" Cleo asked. She had reached Corinne's side before the call ended.

"Why does she want to know if you're not with me? That was one heck of a lie you blew there," Naveen asked.

"Did she tell you where she is?" Julie added, joining in.

Corinne kept quiet and shut out their questions. Nothing made any sense, and she wasn't sure it would make sense to them either. She had to think of a way of presenting it to them.

Naveen had been tossing into his bed once again, not able to sleep. His head ached as if it was going to explode like a volcano, erupting his thoughts everywhere. He was going crazy, thinking, what if Sophie was once again in some trouble. His heart sank every time he thought of the possibility that Sophia might never return to his life again. He asked himself, what if he did not see her ever again? His heart was going to refuse to beat at the mere thought of it. Sophia had now become a part of the cells that ran down his system along with his blood.

He had developed feelings for Drizella after they were married. Several times, he tried to make things better, but once he happened to meet Sophia, he was then introduced to a side of himself that even he had never seen. Sometimes, he felt that the love he had for Sophia was too much, too intense to be carried inside his heart. It was as if his heart had swelled a thousand times more than its normal size so that it could contain all of that love, these strong emotions.

He remembered how he was slowly losing his sanity after seeing Sophia outside the café but did not know how to find her. He had no clue who she was, and he was new to the city; he had no way to locate her, and it was driving him crazy.

For two straight days, he just laid on the couch, staring at the walls and ceiling, not understanding the havoc going on inside of him. It took him quite a while to accept and register the fact into his mind that he had fallen in love at first sight with a girl that he had seen randomly outside a café on a beautiful autumn day. Naveen had never been poetic, but during these few days, he discovered the feeling of finding beauty in the moon and stars.

His phone rang; he sighed before checking who was calling. It was Nikolai, his housekeeper, who had constantly been calling him over the previous two days. Perhaps, he had been expecting Naveen to come back home soon, which Naveen was sure that he was not going to do, at least not until he had found the girl.

It had been a little while after his divorce with Drizella, and he had not been actively dating. He had wholly drowned himself into work. He was not even sure if he would trust any woman at all, but there he was again, head over heels over someone completely strange. What was happening to him?

"Get your shit together, dude," Naveen muttered to himself. "You can't think about having children with a random person you bumped into on the street." He almost laughed out loud at himself, acting like a teenager all of a sudden. He was a mature businessman, and he should have been acting like one.

For the next week, he had gone to the same café at the same time in the hope that he might bump into her again, but there was no luck. By the end of the week, he was hopeless, and it was making him cranky. He had decided to go back home to divert his mind. Drizella had surprisingly not contacted him all week either, so his whole focus was on the stranger girl.

It was two and a half hours before his flight when he left his office and was on his way to the airport when it started raining. Even though he was becoming more poetic those days, the rain ticked him off, seeing the dark clouds showering water on the parched land.

He had called a taxi to drop him off at the airport, but now he was fidgeting in his seat for no reason. Somehow, it was irritating that he was going home when his heart belonged here. With a loud screech, the taxi halted suddenly, throwing him into the air slightly. The driver cursed loudly as the vehicle jolted. For a moment, Naveen could not make out what was happening as even the windscreen was foggy with the rain splattering over it. Then it hit him that the driver in front of them had stopped their car abruptly, which had made his taxi driver follow it.

With the car parked in the middle of the road, it was difficult for them to pass through, and it was annoying the driver, so he had to step out in the rain. He thumped at the window of the car with his fist and said something loudly, which Naveen couldn't understand. He rolled his window down and popped his head out to see what was going on. The last thing that he wanted was to miss his flight.

"Hey, you," the driver thumped again, and Naveen saw the window rolling down and a female voice replying in a shrill voice.

"I am going; I am going." He then heard the engine rev and then dying. The girl was trying to start her car, failing again. The taxi driver was restlessly hovering around, and it was evidently making the girl nervous. Naveen sighed and opened his door to see if he could somehow help.

"Hey, what's wrong?" he asked the driver in a bored tone.

"Hey, hurry!" The driver was thumping the window while the girl opened the door this time and jumped out. The spray of rain-drenched her in seconds, and her hair stuck to her head like a wet chicken. Naveen blinked twice to look at her closely, and his heart nearly stopped.

It was her.

The time seemed to go still. He could even hear his own breathing go shallow.

"I said, I am trying." The girl was annoyed, which brought Naveen back into the moment.

"Hi. May I help you, lady?" he managed to say.

"My car broke down." She slightly pouted, and Naveen realized that he could stare at her all his life. Her hair glued to her head, somewhat annoyed.

"Do you mind if I have a look at your car?" Naveen offered.

The cab driver turned toward him and said, "I thought you had a flight to catch, sir."

Naveen winced and took his wallet out. "I would like to stay back and help this lady. How much?" Without looking at the taxi driver, he gave him a big tip; the driver left with a surprised look on his face.

Naveen, after the driver had left, opened the hood and started checking the car engine.

"Umm, I don't want you to miss your flight. Please, let it be. I will get someone to bring the car to me later," she said, and Naveen shook his head.

"No. The flight is not so important." He wiped his face that was now wet from the rain.

"No, please." The girl was still hesitant.

Naveen looked at her radiant face and suppressed the urge to plant a kiss on her forehead.

"Trust me." He smiled, and she smiled back.

"I am Naveen, by the way." He offered her his hand.

"Sophia," she replied as she shook hands with Naveen. The warmth of her hand sent a shudder down his spine. He had met many women throughout his life, but this kind of effect none of them could manage to have on Naveen.

"Sophia!" He repeated her name and grinned.

"I think your car needs a proper check-up. I will send someone down to pick it up. I know someone who can fix it in minutes." He explained. "I will give him a call. Until then, there is a small coffee joint across the street. Do you mind sitting down and wait there?" He pointed to the coffee place with his finger, and she nodded.

Having butterflies in the stomach was a big understatement; Naveen literally had elephants jumping into his stomach. It was going to be the best evening of his life.

Chapter Seven

Naveen was pacing up and down in a fury and stopped to look at Corinne after a while. "So, you mean to tell me that Sophia is pregnant with 'my child and decided that avoiding me was the next right thing to do?" he said, with a leveled calmness. There was a fire in his eyes, like a mad man. "I can't believe this. This, this is unbelievable! Carrying my child, she decided to run away with it, and to goodness only knows where!" he added, throwing his hands up in angry confusion. "I mean, does it make any sense to any of you?" He was asking no one specifically. "What kind of a woman is she? Does she think I'm irresponsible? Or that I would deny the baby, our baby! This is unbelievable."

"Naveen—" George was going to say something but was immediately interrupted by Naveen.

"No, no, no. Nobody will tell me to calm down. This is simply insane, and right now, all I want to know is where she is and why she is doing this to me? I don't give a rat's ass if anyone of you thinks I'm losing my mind. As a matter of fact, I'm indeed losing it!" Naveen yelled, waving his hands in the air.

"I think she was scared, and she still is," Corinne said quietly.

Naveen barked out a brittle laugh. "Scared of me?"

"No. Scared of your wife, I mean your ex-wife. After what happened, she must have gotten scared when she found out about the baby, and so, she decided to run away. She wasn't embarrassed or scared of you, Naveen; she was just scared of Drizella. In fact, we were all wondering why she was keeping away from all of us. She must have been stuck inside her own head all these days." Corinne was feeling sad for her best friend, who had been running from her own self.

Naveen sank into a chair with his head in his hands. It all made sense now; missing pieces were coming together. As long as Drizella was still around, he was darn sure he couldn't be happy. She would always come back to haunt his happiness and peace; he had suddenly realized that fact.

"I heard a man talking in the background when I spoke with her; he sounded Russian. Could that be a clue?" Corrine suddenly asked, choosing her words carefully.

"Russian?" Naveen asked. It was more of a statement than a question. "Did she use her phone to make the call?"

"No, it…it is an international number."

"Let me see it." There was a little hope in Naveen's voice now. If they knew which country the call came from, they would have a lead to start looking for her.

Naveen suddenly looked shocked as he saw the number, attracting attention from all the others. "Incredible," he said out loud.

"What's the matter? What country is it? Is it nearby?" Cleo asked in a rush.

"I can't believe it," he whispered. "This…this is my number," he said, with a rush of excitement in his voice. He looked at them; he had obviously lost them. "This is my home number! She called from my home number! Sophia is…she's in Vienna! She's at my house in Vienna!"

Everyone went silent as they let it sink in. Sophia was safe; she was home.

Rick looked at him for the umpteenth time. "So, you're going to Vienna?"

"That's obvious," Naveen said, rapping his fingers on the car steering wheel. They had been talking for a while, and Rick still seemed completely confused.

"So, you're going to be a father?" he asked again. Naveen raised his eyebrows at him; over and over, Rick was still asking the same question.

"Really now?" Naveen frowned.

Rick put up his hands in defense. "I'm sorry, it's just. I'm surprised. I find it hard to believe what's happening. I mean, Sophia being so scared of Drizella that she would have to run away?"

Naveen nodded, showing a smile at the corner of his lips. "Drizella has really outdone herself this time. I mean, let's face it. The trauma was bad enough. Now adding my child to the list? Goodness knows what she's done to her this time." Naveen's voice had an edge of bitterness.

"Well, Drizella seemed repentant." Rick shrugged.

"You really want me to believe that cock and bull story she told you about feeling sorry? It's Drizella, for heaven's sake! Tell me tigers could go from orange to pink, and I'd believe it, but Drizella? Never. She can never change."

"Well, I think—"

"Why are you suddenly acting like her lawyer? Did she bribe you to convince me?" Naveen asked half humorously.

"I'd prefer taking a bungee jump off the Everest than accepting a bribe from her." Rick scoffed. "Anyways, thanks for dropping me off at home," he said as he opened the door. He looked thoughtful for a while. "Congratulations, Naveen." He stretched his hand to shake his, smiling now.

"You know you give me the heebie-jeebies when you're formal, so cut it out. Congratulations to you too; you're going to be a godfather." Rick laughed at this.

"Well, find her first and pray she hasn't fled before you get to Vienna."

"Thanks for the heads up; I'll see you when I get back."

"I'll be right here, ironing my best suit," he replied with a grin, smiling even bigger as Naveen drove off. He was really happy for Naveen.

"Godfather, yeah? Cool." Rick grinned and walked inside the house.

The flight felt too long, way longer than all the other times he had gone to Vienna before. He kept fidgeting in his seat and checking his watch until he had to remove it in exasperation. "Can this thing go any faster?" he muttered under his breath over and over again. He tried to sleep, but he couldn't. He was excited and scared at the same time. When the plane finally touched the ground, he heaved a huge sigh of relief. "Finally," he whispered to himself. He boarded a taxi rather than calling home, so nobody would know he was coming. His heartbeat went crazy as he got closer to the house.

The house was no different than when he had left it. Beautiful yellow and orange flowers had bloomed, and the lawn had been freshly mowed, but other than that, nothing had changed. The taxi driver parked the car outside to let him out. He really hoped she was still there, afraid of what might happen if she knew he was coming; she could be on the run again, and this time maybe without a trace.

Nikolai was leaning against the kitchen door, watching her lying on the couch. Nothing he had told her would make her change her mind; he had never met a more strong-headed woman, stubborn perhaps.

"What if he finds out you're here?" he had asked Sophia.

"Unless you tell him, he won't find out." she had replied., curling a tendril of hair around her finger.

Nikolai shook his head; he knew it was only a matter of time before Naveen found out where she was hiding; he just didn't know how long it would take. The doorbell rang. He moved away and went to get the door. One would say he looked shocked, to say the least, when seeing Naveen appearing at the door. "Boss? Sir, you—"

"Surprised to see me? Why would that be? It's not the first time I'm coming to my house unannounced, is it?" he said knowingly, smiling with relief.

"No, well…" Nicholai began.

"Why are you standing in my way? Move aside, Nikolai." Naveen said, pushing him away. "Where is she?"

"Who, sir? she…"

Naveen turned around, eyes flashing, masking his fear with his anger. "She what?"

"On the couch." he pointed. "Sir, she made me promise not to tell you." He was now wondering how he would manage to keep his job, not knowing what was on Naveen's mind. He looked mad, and the last thing Nikolai wanted was to direct the anger toward him.

"She did, didn't she?" Naveen said with sarcasm as he strode toward the couch. It was when he saw her. She looked fearless in her sleep, a calm on her face as though she had no worries. Naveen squatted and played with a loose strand of her hair.

Sophia stirred, and her eyes flew open. She sat up immediately, her eyes widening in shock and then fear. "You?" she almost stammered. She was not hoping to see him.

"Me." He said coolly.

"What are you doing here?" She questioned, her eyes flickering as she stared at Nikolai. Now she was mad, too.

"I came to get you." Naveen smiled.

She rolled her eyes and stood up, "I didn't want to see you." She tried to walk past him.

He caught her by the wrist. "Lies," he said, standing up.

"How did you learn I was here?" she asked in a tone that reflected anger. He didn't seem fazed. And what was with the stupid calm look on his face? Did he not know how unnerving it was? "Nikolai, you—"

"I didn't tell him anything!" Nikolai said hurriedly, still scared about losing his job. They were both going to be angry with him, and he didn't want that.

"This is my house." He said, "You called with my number."

Shoot! How could she have been so careless? "But I called Corinne—" Her hand flew to her forehead.

"Lied to you. I apologize on her behalf. We were all at your house when you called. Did you really think she would hide such a thing from me? She would not tell me such an important thing simply because you told her not to? Just like you made Nikolai not tell me anything, do you think she wouldn't?" His voice was rising.

"Let me go, Naveen!" she said, struggling against his grip.

"No. I'm not letting you run away from me again. Not today, not ever," he said. "Not anymore." His voice was cold and razor-sharp. He was frustrated; why won't she let him love her in peace?

"Naveen…"

"Did you at any time stop to think about how worried sick everyone would be? You know how your mom gets when she's worried, and you thought running away was the best solution? Didn't you care how everyone would feel? You only thought about yourself!" Naveen's eyes blazed.

"I had no choice!" she yelled.

"You had a choice!" he replied with matching decibels. "You had a choice Sophia; you could have told someone. We all kept wondering what was wrong, and the whole time you were thinking about how to disappear without a trace. Did you not think about how I would feel?"

"It was the only way—"

"It was a silly way. You're carrying my child Sophia, our child. You could have told me." His voice was less loud and less angry. She fell silent. She sank slowly into the couch.

"I was scared!" she replied, quivering. "It all happened so fast. The kidnaping, everything Drizella did and said to me while I was under her grip. And when I found out I was carrying your child, the only thing I could think of…." Her throat felt as if on fire as she began to shed tears. Her body started shaking as she cried; she covered her face with her hands.

"Drizella," he said quietly, sitting next to her.

"What did she say to you?" Naveen asked, rubbing her knee.

She turned herself away. "You are married, Naveen."

"Lies. She told you lies. I was married."

"To her."

"Yes, but we're divorced. She just wants to get back at me for something I didn't do. Believe me, Sophia, I'm speaking the truth; I'm no longer married to her. I want to spend the rest of my life with you. I love you, and only you."

Sophia shut her eyes and shook her head like a little child.

"Look at me, Sophia, please," he said, begging.

"Naveen...."

"Marry me, Sophia." He got off the couch and went on his knees in front of her. His eyes were shimmering with tears. His emotions were too intense to be contained in his heart anymore.

She shook her head. "It is not that easy. Our lives are way too complicated, Naveen."

"It won't be unless you let it be. Just say yes." He then put his hands on her knees.

"It's not so easy." She sobbed.

"It is, and you know it is. Be mine forever. No more running away or fears about Drizella."

She wanted to believe him, she wanted to tell him she trusted him, she wanted to say she loved him, and a million other things, but her voice betrayed her. Instead, she wept, realizing that she really didn't have to run. No matter where she would hide, he would always find her. She would always have a family back home to turn to if things went awry. She had her stepfather, who made missing her biological father, less hurtful. Her mom simply couldn't bear seeing her in pain. Her sister, playing in her hair every time she could, but still so adorable. A best friend she would never trade for pounds of gold. And a man who would go crazy if anything ever happened to her, a man she loved with every fiber of her being. She had everything, and she wanted to tell him that much. But she couldn't find her voice, not today.

"Will you marry me?" he asked again. But this time, she nodded. "Yes!"

Naveen laughed as his eyes let out the tears that were lingering inside them. He cupped her face and touched his forehead with hers; he was run out of words.

A few days later

Corinne looked up from cleaning the tables when she heard a deep voice. The coffee shop was closed for the rest of the day, and Leela had gone home, as they were no more expecting customers. The face was familiar, but the person had dark glasses on, so she wasn't sure.

"Corinne Martinez?" the stranger asked.

She walked toward him. "Yes, that's me. How may I help you? We're closed for the day, you—"

"I haven't come for coffee, though I must admit you have a beautiful place. It is very lovely," the man added, looking around.

"Who are you, if I may ask?" Corinne replied, finding it hard to remember where she had seen him.

"You really don't remember me, Corinne?" the man said, taking a few steps closer until he was standing right before her. "Think Martinez. Do you really not remember me?" he asked again, taking off his glasses. She stared into his blue eyes, and then it hit her all of a sudden.

"You..." She covered her mouth with her hand in total surprise. "Trent. It's you?" Seeing Trent again was the last thing she could ever think of. She stepped back. "But... You..." She put her hand to her forehead. "I can't believe this," she whispered. She looked at him again, shock and disbelief revealed on her face.

"I'm back," he said, with his baritone voice.

"After all these years. How did you know where I was? And where is my daughter?" was the only other thing she could ask, her face a mix of surprise, pain, and anger.

"I looked for you. I've been looking all over for you these past three years."

"Well, now you have found me; good for you. And as you can see, I'm doing fine. So, where is my daughter?" she snapped in a razor-sharp tone.

"I've come back for you, Corinne," he said, his tone pleading and apologetic. He moved toward her, but she raised her hand to stop him from getting any closer.

"You've come back, really? So, what? What should I do about it? You think you can run off and then come back after all these years, stroll into my place, and then I'll run into your arms?"

"Corinne…"

"Other than my daughter, I don't want to have anything to do with you. And for the last time, where is she?" Corinne was almost yelling.

"Janessa misses you," he said after a pause. He could see her anger soften.

"You took her away from me, Trent. You took my daughter away from me." She sobbed.

"I did not. You don't know what happened. You should stop accusing me! There was an accident, our ship was wrecked, but we survived miraculously."

Corinne struggled with whether this was the truth or not. Was he telling her the truth or looking for a way to get on her good side? "How do you expect me to believe you?" she elevated her chin stubbornly.

"Because this is the truth," Trent replied. He had closed the distance and held her by the shoulder. "We survived, our daughter and I. Believe me, Corinne, I've been looking for you ever since I was able to stand on my feet again."

She rolled her eyes. "Do you realize that I've lived all these years thinking you were dead, only to see your photos in the papers one day? What kind of a man leaves his wife and disappears with their daughter, and waltzes in one fine winter night and—"

"I'm sorry, Corinne; I'm sorry. I know I was away for so long; it is difficult to comprehend. Will you forgive me, please? For us, for Janessa." He said with his blue eyes imploring.

She shook her head. "Where is Janessa?" She looked at him for a long time; she could see the truth in his eyes. He was still the same, only a little different; his face looked older with a few worry lines.

She sighed deeply. "I need to hear the whole story..." she began.

"But..."

"And see Janessa." she insisted firmly. "Before I can decide whether or not to forgive you. What is it going to be, Trent?"

He looked at her and smiled a little. God, had he missed her? The old stubbornness was still there. She had built a tougher skin over the years, no doubt, but he could still recognize his wife beneath all these layers, the little girl he had fallen madly in love with and married. It was all there, behind the strong casing, it was all there, and he would give it all it took to win her heart all over again. "Fine. No problem. But get ready to travel; we're going to Mexico."

She folded her arms and nodded firmly. If that meant getting her family back, then so it would be.

It was sunny…very pleasantly sunny. She was lying under the sun, with the warmth of the beams caressing her skin. She had her eyes closed as she soaked in the sun and peace around. She could smell flowers of many different kinds. She tried to guess which one smelt the best or at least name one or two of them.

Wild angelica? She remembered what that sweet, almost vanilla-like scent must be. Whatever it was; was pushing her into a deep and peaceful slumber. She inhaled and gulped a large amount of fresh air to fill her lungs. Her hair danced with the wind; she softly ran her fingers in them. "Buzz, buzz, buzz." Something buzzed in her ear. "UGH, Go away, you." She shook her head violently and then waved her hand around her face and head to shoo it away.

It was when she heard a giggling; delicious and sweet. It belonged to a child, a very happy child. She popped her eyes open and slowly sat up to find herself in a meadow. It was lush green and bright, as you see in pictures and wallpapers. The sun shone brightly, and white clouds floated freely like cotton buds. She sat in a state of mesmerism until she heard the giggling again. She craned her neck to look around and saw a tall man carrying a child on his broad shoulders, who was actually the source of the giggling. They had their backs toward her and were looking at something far away.

The little girl had dark curly hair, which danced as the wind danced, exactly like hers.

"Daddy, a dandelion." She pointed her tiny finger at a flower bed, and her father turned. His perfect teeth gleamed as he smiled broader at the flower bed first and then turned his head to look at her.

"Mommy, look." The kid waved at her, and she looked at them. "Naveen?" She smiled. He also waved at her. "Naveen!" someone yelled, but it was not her. They all looked at the person calling his name, and there she was with a gun in her hand. "Drizella, stop!"

Before she could even move, the gun fired. The bang was so loud that the birds nesting in the meadows flew off, and then there was silence.

Sophia then woke up, her heart thumping madly in her chest. She tried to calm herself. "It was just a dream; it was just a dream." She rocked herself, but the tears wouldn't stop.

The table lamp switched on, and Naveen wrapped his arms around her quivering body. "What's wrong, sweetheart? Sophia?" He put her head on his chest while she sobbed hard.

Naveen sighed, and his hatred for Drizella amplified. He had to deal with her once and for all.

Chapter Eight

One month later.

Naveen was driving his car into the garage, nodding to a song playing in his head. He had been in a state of bliss ever since he had found out about the baby. Pulling the car aside, he looked at Sophia; she had been silent throughout the entire drive. Now, whenever she was not talking, it worried Naveen a lot. Who knew she might be planning to run away again?

"What's the matter, Soph?" Naveen asked her in a gentle voice.

"Nothing," she said quietly and started looking out of the window to avoid making eye contact with Naveen.

"Sophia, nothing means something. What is bothering you?" he asked, his voice laced with concern. "Are you feeling okay?"

"I'm fine, Naveen, really." He got out of the car and hurried to the other side to open the door for her. "Naveen, I promise, I'm fine." She emphasized each word. She hated that whatever she did would scare Naveen these days.

They walked toward the house silently for a while. "Didn't you like the party?" he tried again.

"No, the party was lovely, it was really nice, and Janessa is such a sweet little angel," she said, smiling a little. Her best friend had found her family, and Sophia could not be happier.

"You're still surprised, aren't you? I have to hand it to Trent though, that reunion party was classic. I'm happy for them." Naveen shoved his hands in the pockets of his trousers and sighed.

"And so am I. I'm happy for Corinne. She finally got her blissful ending. I mean, a lot of people did not even know she was married," she said, looking at Naveen now, not looking lost or the worried Sophia.

"Neither did I," he replied. "She didn't look or act that way. For a woman of her age, she seems way younger. I'll admit it; I was blown away to learn she was both married and had a daughter."

"She's just 28, Naveen. Not as old as you are thinking," Sophia added, sighing as they reached the door.

"Well, while she's at the end of her twenties and you're two years younger, you both have many different personalities. In the end, still, she will have done well for herself." He rang the doorbell and waited.

"For a moment, I was worried for her, but seeing that glow on both her face and Trent's, I had to convince myself that this was it. This time, Corinne could have a family to call hers, and everything would be alright." The door opened, with Frances smiling at them both. He slightly nodded as he looked at them.

"You're back so soon! How was the party?"

"It was lovely, Frances. I wish you had come," Sophia said.

"Now, now, you know how the saying goes. Three is a crowd."

"Frances," She widened her eyes at her.

"I'm just kidding, dear child. Come in now; the weather is quite cold. I'll bring you tea."

"No thanks, I'm fine. I don't know about Naveen, but I'm fine."

"Same here. Thanks, Frances. Have a good night."

She regarded them curiously. "Alright then, good night," she said hesitantly and left them after locking the door.

There was an awkward lingering silence before Naveen finally spoke. "Sophia-" he started, pulling her into his arms. "I know you're worried about your friend, but you and I both know that she deserves the best. I feel she will be fine. They will be fine." She sighed and rested her head on his chest, listening to his heartbeat, which always sounded familiar. "Sophia, worrying doesn't suit you. I don't want you to overthink things. Everything will be fine," he assured her.

She looked up at him, the corner of her lips curved into a smile. "Tell me, gorgeous Naveen, how not to worry?"

He raised his eyebrows at the request, not really understanding her. He smiled after a while and bent a little lower, kissing her slowly. "Even though I don't fully understand what you mean, instead of telling you," he said, wriggling off her coat, "why don't I show you?" He removed her hair clip and let her hair fall loosely behind her.

"Please do," she giggled as he carried her in his arms, up the stairs, and into their bedroom. The moonlight was letting itself through the curtains and gave the room rows of silvery beauty. Watching her stand against the illumination from the moon, he thought he had never seen anything more beautiful. He took his time to savor her beauty before he delicately started undressing her. To him, she was like a package of endless loveliness, which would take him forever to unwrap, as he wished to explore every inch of her body with his heart full of love for her.

"I love you so much, Sophia," he whispered into her ear through the curtain of her thick hair.

She smiled as she took off the last piece of clothing he had on him. "I love you more, Naveen."

With him, she knew there wouldn't be any more worries, not today, and hopefully, not ever. Everything would be fine, as long as they had each other to hold on to.

Corinne was waiting as Trent shut the door quietly behind him. He looked up at her, and for a moment, she thought she caught his eye twinkling. He had just come from Janessa's bedroom.

"She's asleep," he said quietly, moving toward her. "Tired?" he asked as he snaked his arms around her waist and pulled her closer. With gentle hands, he started making small circles around the back of her neck.

"Not so much. Maybe a little. But I enjoyed the party," she sheepishly said as she snuggled against him. Trent was well-built with a slightly wide upper body, and she liked it that way. She was smaller than he was, so he could easily engulf her in his embrace. His chest vibrated as he spoke. This was funny to her and a bit ticklish, but she was relishing the moment, still thinking about how much she had missed him, missed his comforting voice, his belly laughter, and his unmatchable cooking skills. She missed the skillful way he flipped pancakes and served them with his favorite Canadian maple syrup and wild blueberries. He had a friend who owned a sugar shack in the deep rural region of Beauce in Quebec, and he had promised her they would make it over there together, so she could enjoy the best maple treats she could ever dream of. And she had missed the way his voice went off-key whenever he sang with headphones on.

"You're quiet. What are you thinking about?" he asked, not releasing the embrace but slowly running his fingers in her hair now.

"You," she said, turning her face to look up at him. "I'm thinking about you. About us. The way it all was, and how I've missed you, Trent Martinez."

"Corinne," he said, leaning toward her in a way he could rest his chin on her shoulder. "Corinne, I know we've had a lot of hard moments over the years, but I want you to know that I am now here to stay. Forever. I'm not leaving you again. I will remain by your side. I can promise you that, with my life," he said as he planted a kiss in her hair.

"Oh, Trent," she said, her voice almost a silent sob as she stood on tiptoes to hug him with all of the might she could collect. "Thanks for coming back to me."

"I never meant to leave," he said, his voice husky with visible emotion. They stayed in a silent embrace for a while, with intense thoughts reeling through their heads. Trent buried his face in her light-colored mass of silky hair; his warm breath on her scalp made Corinne's skin prickle. She was back on her feet so that she could shift slightly. He tucked a loose strand of hair behind her ear and kissed her temple softly. Her silver sequin gown was sleeveless, so he could easily draw a feathery line down her arms, nibbling playfully on her neck. He was only a few inches taller than she was, so he didn't have to bend so much. He drew a line of kisses down her throat and stopped where her gown's plunging heart-shaped neckline stopped. He went back to her face, kissing her forehead and the bridge of her nose, to finally tease the corner of her lips.

"I love the way you danced at the party," he said, with slight humor in his tone. He was being deliberate about tormenting her this way. Turning her on until she would not be able to take it anymore while letting her know he wasn't going to be rushed. He would take his time, a patient lover he was. He made circular motions on her belly, depositing a teasing kiss on the other side of her lip. He knew how delicate she was and which part of her body was the most sensitive. And apparently, he had not forgotten. Her stomach tightened in reflex.

"Trent," she whispered as her legs touched the bedpost. She did not know whether he was moving too fast or moving too slow, leaving her head spinning. He played with her hair and removed the fancy clip that held it upswept.

"I love it when your hair is let down like this. You look like a goddess and a queen all in one," he said, taking out the last bobby pin. "Your beauty is enchanting." He was picking his words carefully, doing a slow mental countdown from one hundred. He held the side of her face. Her eyes were hazy. Had there been a scoreboard, he would have gained big points. He brought his face close to her and watched her eyes flutter shut. He kissed her, lightly at first, almost in a feathery way. Then, he slowly deepened his kiss until his tongue found hers. Her hand came up to his face, and she started tickling him inside his ear. He fought hard to suppress a groan; he was supposed to be the one leading on the scoreboard. He had almost forgotten that she knew him almost as well as he knew her.

"You want to drive me crazy, Corinne," he said quietly against her face.

"You're already driving me crazy. So, let's get even," she replied in a tone that only told him the scoreboard was increasing in his favor. He found the tiny buttons behind her gown and skillfully undid them one after the other. "This dress suits you perfectly," he purred in her ear.

"And so, does this shirt." Only then did he realize she was halfway gone with his buttons as she wrested the shirt out of his trousers.

It could have been competition between both of them as winners, but they were two love birds, lost in the ecstasy of each other, with their hearts beating, one for the other. As they drank in each other's beauty and reached heights and depths, once again, love blossomed. A ravaging fire that an ocean could not put out. In their hearts for each other, this fire crackled with just a tone that echoed 'forever.'

Corinne stirred awake at night, feeling uneasy. She turned on the bedside lamp and looked at the little clock on the table. The clock read 3:05 a.m. She got out of bed and stretched. She looked at Trent snoring softly and smiled as he looked so cute sleeping. She looked around and felt something wrong. She had this uneasy feeling something was not right, even though everything seemed normal. She went toward the bedroom door, silently opened it, and stepped out of the room. She waited for a moment but heard nothing. Instinctively, she went toward Janessa's room and opened the door. She switched on the lights and stood motionless, staring in confusion. Janessa looked still for a moment and then made a sound as though gasping for breath.

Corinne hurried over to her. "Janessa! Darling. Are you okay, Janessa?" she shouted. She put her hand to her forehead; it was burning hot, and her breathing was shallow. Her sheets were wet, and Corinne realized that Janessa had been throwing up in her bed. She shook her gently in her arms, but her eyes would not open. She hopped off the bed and ran to her room, opening the door with a loud bang.

"Trent!" she yelled, making him fly up in shock. He hopped out of bed, with the duvet tangling around him.

"What? What? Is there a fire?" he said hurriedly, looking around frantically. Corinne looked at him for a moment and realized she had actually called him as if there were a fire.

"No, Trent, there's no fire."

"Gracious! Why did you have to call my name like that? I could have gotten a heart attack!"

"I'm sorry! I didn't mean to. It's Janessa, she…she has a fever. She can't breathe properly, and she's really burning up. I don't know why, and she's not opening her eyes. You need to come with me."

He detangled the duvet and went after her, as she had already left the room. He touched Janessa's forehead.

"You're right. Let's get her to the emergency. I'll put on something."

"What do you think could be the cause? Why would she have a fever," Corinne asked before he could leave the room.

Trent paused for a second and looked at her. "I don't know, Corinne. A germ probably, or…I don't know. I'm a first-class chef, Corinne, not a doctor. So, I'll go get dressed, and then we can take her to the hospital where they should know better why she has a fever. Alright?" he said, one thing after the other so that she could register it all properly.

"I have an awful feeling about this, Trent," she said worriedly.

Trent walked over to her to pull her in a side embrace. "Listen, I know you're worried, but I promise you that we will do all it takes to make sure she gets better. It can only be a fever. The doctors will do whatever they have to do, and she'll be fine. Alright? Plus, I think you should get dressed too. We don't know how long we'll have to wait. You don't want people coming in the morning and see you in your nightdress. Come on, let's go get dressed."

"Alright," she said, with doubt and fear in her voice. She could feel deep down that something was not right. She looked over her shoulder at Janessa one more time before they both left the room.

Corinne looked through the glass in the door at Janessa, lying in her hospital bed. They were lucky, the doctor had said; food poisoning was the main reason behind the fever, and it could have been fatal had they not come when they did.

Food poisoning seemed to make no sense to Corinne. Everything used and eaten at the party had been made with fine ingredients by top-class, perfectly clean chefs. Food poisoning could not then have been the problem. But it was, as per the test results. The question then was how. Every reasonable and seemingly logical explanation she had come up within her head didn't seem to fit. She was herself fine, Trent was fine, everyone else seemed to be fine, and nobody had called to complain. She felt a hand on her shoulder and looked back; it was Trent.

He opened his arms to hug her, and she went straight into them and sighed heavily. Trent smiled above her head. It was sporadic to see Corinne in such a scared and frazzled state. He could almost see engines in her head working so furiously and tirelessly trying to find out what had really happened.

"Duchess Martinez," he said, teasing her. "You will simply overwork those poor neurons in your head until they decide not to work anymore. Give them a break, will you? They need sugar, and you haven't eaten anything since yesterday."

"I'm just confused, Trent," she said, with evident exasperation.

"As am I. It beats me, as well. I just don't get it. But listen to me." He stepped back a bit and tilted up her head to look at him. "You're my superwoman; you're strong, you're beautiful, you have a large heart full of endless love and many invisible hands to do so many things simultaneously. Our Janessa is just like you, Corinne. She's beautiful, and she's strong too. She'll pull through. People with strong and beautiful hearts like yours are fighters. Our girl will be just fine."

Corinne smiled a little more brightly. "You have to be right," she finally said.

A few hours later, Janessa woke up and was stable enough to answer questions. She looked at both her parents as she sat up in her bed, both legs crossed in yoga style. She put her little hand on Corinne's cheek and then looked at Trent, saying, "Mommy's looking tired."

"She is a sweetheart," Trent smiled at her.

"And so are you, only a little less glumpy than mommy," she observed.

Trent stood up from his chair and sat beside her, asking, "Glumpy? Or grumpy?"

"No, not grumpy. Glumpy. You know, from glum and grumpy," she said innocently.

Trent raised his eyebrows in amusement. "Glumpy. Hmm, that's a new word to add to our big dictionary. Don't you think so, Corinne?"

Corinne nodded, "Absolutely." There was silence for a while, and then Janessa looked at Corinne again.

"I'm sorry, mommy," she said sadly.

Corinne's head came up. "Why? What are you sorry for, darling?"

"You didn't get to sleep because of me," the little girl replied, looking down.

"Hey," Corinne stated while sitting at the other side of her daughter's bed. "You don't have to feel bad about it. Mom and Dad are just worried about you, that's all. But now that you're fine, we feel better already," she said with a smile, playfully pulling her daughter's cheek while looking to Trent for support.

"Yes, princess. We were worried about you, but you're fine now, and the doctor said we could take you home very soon."

Janessa looked at both of them, she may just be six, but she had sharp eyes and an even sharper brain. They could have forgotten for a moment that she was a combination of both of them, but little as she was, she knew they were still worried.

"Mommy." She tried again. "Promise you're okay."

Corinne was stunned. Had she really become that transparent, or was she simply being paranoid, and it showed too much. "I promise you, darling, I am."

"Pinky promise," she said, raising her little finger. She looked at Trent, who only grinned, like the cat that just ate the canary.

"Yes, Janessa. Pinkie promise," Corinne said eventually, touching Janessa's little finger with hers.

The tense atmosphere lessened a bit, and they started communicating more easily. What also helped was Trent making animal sounds and funny faces, to which both ladies could not hold their laughter. Next, he was a pirate and then a magician, and then a knight in rusty armor.

They both laughed so heartily and fearlessly that they did not notice the face of a man at the door, looking through the glass. Had they happened to look up, they would have seen him and the angry scowl on his face.

Corinne suddenly felt the need to use the toilet, and as she looked up at the door, she was almost sure she saw someone move away. She did not really pay any attention to it. After all, there were dozens of people walking along the corridor. However, she had a nudge that the person had been watching through the door. She excused herself and was about to leave the room when Janessa's statement stopped her.

"You know a very nice gentleman gave me a lollipop at the party," she quipped innocently. Corinne turned around and saw that Trent also had the same confused look.

"Who?" Corinne asked.

"He said his name was Frank, and that he was daddy's friend from a long time ago, and that he was going to pay him a visit soon."

Trent had never been more confused. He had no friend named Frank, much less an old friend. He remembered everyone he had been friends with from high school to college, and then culinary school, and none of them had the name Frank, not even his teachers. He decided to probe further.

"Really? How nice of him. What did he look like? I can't seem to remember him so much. Did he have big googly eyes and donkey ears?" he asked in a funny voice and shrugged when Corinne gave him a look that said: "Really? Big googly eyes" He thought he had to try.

The little girl chuckled. "No. he had shiny black hair like a mouse's eyes and a little wart on his nose," she said. Corinne's mouth twisted in suppressed laughter. Who compares someone's hair to a mouse's eyes? "Oh, and the front of his hair is a bit curly; it doesn't stay with the rest of his hair."

Trent was even more confused. None of the descriptions matched. Neither did it ring a bell. He had done a mental 'friend database scan,' and all the faces had no warts and slick hair.

He thought about it at night after they had gotten home with Janessa from the hospital. There was a probable answer. The poisoning had not come from the food but from the lollipop given by the mysterious fellow who claimed to be his friend. The question hung ominously. Why would anyone in his right state of mind want to poison his daughter, an innocent little girl? Of course, Janessa had learned to be wary of strangers, but everyone in the party was 'Daddy and Mommy's friends,' so he could not blame her for letting her guard down.

"You really do not have a friend called Frank?" Corinne asked.

"No. You know all my friends. So, you tell me."

"Could he be someone you met during the last three years?"

"No, Janessa and I were in Mexico. There was no Frank, and certainly none with slick hair," he said, getting worn out thinking.

"Do you believe he might be responsible for what happened to Janessa?"

"My best guess is, he couldn't be my friend and then give my daughter a poisoned lollipop. That would just not make any sense. We know there is no way she could have been poisoned through the food. She was with us all through the party and even ate from Sophia's plate. And so far, Naveen has not called with bad news about Sophia being sick. He did call to thank us for the party and to wish us good luck. So, it was not the food."

"I think you're right. Something is fishy. You know me, Trent, I'm not a paranoid person, but I definitely know someone is up to something. I think we need to involve the police."

"You're right. I will contact them tomorrow. It's infuriating just thinking about it. My headaches already," he groaned and adjusted the pillow under his head as he shut his eyes.

"Anything I can do to make you feel better?" Corinne asked with mastered coyness. He opened one eye to look at her and then the other.

"Come here," he said finally. She moved closer to him and placed her head on his chest. She could hear his heartbeat in a confused frenzy. No one had the right to treat her family this way, and she would do all she can to unmask the crook behind everything. Her first plan for the next day was to speak with Sophia. She needed the time out and girl time brainstorming.

Dear God, she prayed inwardly, *please keep my family safe from this guy, whoever he is.*

Sophia turned around in bed most of the night, as she could not sleep. She had had this strange feeling since she and Naveen had returned from Trent and Corinne's reunion party. She had felt restless throughout the day and had contained herself to not snap at Naveen when he would not stop asking what was wrong. Even she didn't know what was wrong. She called the boutique to tell her assistant she would not be coming. She had dressed up to go to her parents and had stopped halfway, going back home instead. And with Julie back to school, there wasn't so much she wanted to tell her mother anyways. She had been to Corinne's coffee shop and found out she wasn't there and called her home line, but no one picked up, meaning they were not in. She simply thought they had gone out on a family outing. Naveen had called from work to ask if she wanted to go out for lunch, but she didn't feel like it, so she had said no. She had picked at the food Frances had prepared, and after a few bites, she said she was full and went upstairs.

She turned the entire day over in her mind and could not make much sense of it. It was unlike her to be like that, but she simply could not place her finger on it. Why was she so worried about Corinne? This was something she could not conjure an explanation for. Naveen was asleep, but she was as wide awake as she could be. She decided on one thing: she would call Corinne in the morning.

Corinne and Sophia had a strange relationship. They were not sisters, but as they say, some ties are stronger than your blood ties, and their relationship was one of the same nature. Sophia could never imagine living a day without seeing Corinne, or even if they did not see each other every day, they would make sure that they talk over the phone or messages. They just had to stay connected somehow. They had been friends for the past ten years. They went to college together, even when Corinne was two years older than Sophia, but due to a shortage of funds, she had to give her education a break for two years. After graduating from college, Corinne had decided to go to culinary school while Sophia pursued fashion designing.

While they were going to different institutes, they managed to see each other during their breaks. Sophia knew that Corinne had met Trent in her culinary class and had been going out with him for a couple of months, but when she had told her that she was getting married, Sophia had been taken aback a little.

Corinne was 22 and a half, not even 23. She had a long life ahead, not forgetting her dream of setting up her own chain of restaurants. Sophia had never been against getting married; in fact, she loved the idea of spending one's life with someone you loved but not like that. She had sat Corinne down and talked about it.

They were sitting on their favorite spot at the lake while they watched children play. It was a warm evening, people soaking the sun and enjoying the summer.

"I am very happy for you, Corinne. Really. I am thrilled to be your bridesmaid, too, but have you thought it through?" Sophia asked her as she handed her a lemonade.

"I love Trent." Corinne smiled and took a sip from the plastic glass. Her eyes were lingering on the kids playing in front of them.

"I know, but are you sure?" Sophia struggled to choose her words carefully as the last thing she wanted was to give Corinne the impression that she was not happy for her. "You think you can give up your dream of opening your restaurant?"

"No, Soph. The best thing about him, apart from the fact that he loves me madly, is that we are in the same business. He will always support me in fulfilling my dream." Corinne frowned. She understood that Sophia was worried about her, but she had never seen it that way. Getting married never meant she had to give up her dreams.

"I am sure that he would," Sophia said, smiling tightly and sipping her lemonade. At this point, she had realized that Corinne had made up her mind, and there was no going back once she had reached that point. Corinne was a strong-headed woman, and Sophia guessed that she knew what she was doing.

"Soph, do you like kids?" Corinne suddenly asked Sophia, slightly turning toward her to see her reaction.

"Umm, I don't know. It depends," Sophia replied, shrugging.

"Depends on what?" Corinne was biting her lip to suppress her smile.

"On how long I am watching them." Sophia giggled. "I can keep up for a while, I assume. Not forever, though."

"Would you like to have children? I mean not now, but once you are ready?"

"I don't have a clue where this conversation is going, but yeah, I think so," Sophia said, with a puzzled look on her face.

"How would you like it if I asked you to choose between being my bridesmaid or a godmother?" Corinne was leaning a little, so she was now half laying on the grass, balancing her weight on her elbows.

"What does that even mean? I can't be both?" Sophia pouted. "Plus, there is plenty of time in becoming the godmother anyways." She imitated Corinne as she laid on the grass with her.

"Who knows?" Corinne looked at the sky and grinned. Sophia went still, like a statue.

"You gotta be shitting me. Tell me you're joking, Corinne." Sophia instantly sat up, her eyes wide as saucers.

Corinne smiled mischievously and shook her head. "What? Noooo!" Sophia jumped to hug her awkwardly. "You are pregnant?" It was more of an accusation than a question. As Corinne nodded, they both had burst into tears. They hugged each other for a long time and cried their eyes out, sometimes giggling for no apparent reason. Some people gave them strange looks, but they could have hardly cared even if a dinosaur showed up running toward them. They were in their own bubble of bliss.

For the next few days, Sophia had relived the moment in her head and smiled. Happy was a word too small what she felt for Corinne. All her fears and worries she had for Corinne had disappeared, as in a puff of smoke it seemed. The only thing that mattered to Sophia was that Corinne would now have the family she had always wanted.

Corinne had lost her parents at a very young age and had grown up in the foster care system. A family was something she had always yearned for. Even though she was always welcome in Sophia's, she wanted to have her own family. Sophia was grateful to Trent that he had brought this massive sac of happiness to her sister-like friend.

They had decided to get married before the baby arrived. They exchanged vows on the same spot at the lake, under the stars. Sophia helped Corinne plan everything. The wedding was traditional and simple, with a minimal guest list. Trent's family was present, along with Sophia's family, as they were all that Corinne had. Trent had kissed her as soon as they were done with the vows, and with the way Corinne had laughed then, Sophia knew that she was going to be alright, for her whole life.

Four weeks later, Sophia and Trent were planning a surprise baby shower for Corinne on the same spot as they had received the scan reports that showed that a baby girl was on her way. They could not contain their excitement and joy, so they decided to throw an early baby shower. Sophia felt her heart expanded each time she looked at Corinne and Trent. The way they were looking forward to welcoming the baby. Sophia secretly hoped that when it was her turn to become a mother, her partner would be as happy as Trent was.

Time had flown as if it had wings, changing warm evening to savagely cold nights. One of those chilly nights, Sophia got a message from Trent with a picture in which he and Corinne held their tiny bundle of joy. It was early in the morning, and Sophia wished she could visit her god-daughter immediately, but it was snowing, so she had to wait until a little later.

Sophia had never known before the emotions that little Janessa could stir inside her heart. She had met and held babies, but this little one was different; it was her god-daughter, and she held a special place inside her heart.

They had celebrated Janessa's birth for months, each time bringing her presents as they visited her. Corinne was a proud mother, as the perfect little version of her gave her a sense of glory whenever she would look at her. Perhaps, that was a parent thing.

Sophia enjoyed seeing Janessa a lot, who had a well-defined personality from the day she was born. She had a serious but cute look on her beautiful face. Trent jokingly called her prematurely mature. One could easily tell how she was a very intelligent kid from the beginning.

Life went on like that for a while until Trent had to attend a funeral in his family in Italy. He insisted that he took Janessa with him as his family wanted to see her. At first, Corinne did not want to let them go without her, but since she had a restaurant to run, she had to let them go on their own. Trent promised that he would take good care of Janessa. He booked his tickets to Palermo, saying he would also have to take a small cruise ride to reach the small town his family was now living in. Sophia had gone with Corinne to see Trent and Janessa off at the airport. It would be the last time they would see them.

Days turned into weeks and weeks into months, but still, there was no news from Trent. In the beginning, Sophia was afraid that Corinne would drive herself insane as she struggled to try to trace them, always without success. She tried reaching every contact number and everyone that Trent had ever introduced her to, but nobody knew where he had gone.

Sophia had decided to move in with Corinne until she got better, but she could not stop her tears when Corinne would wake up and cry out loud for her baby in the middle of the night. Time is a healer, as they had heard, and Corinne slowly got better. She wrapped her heart with steel armor and finally got stronger and better each day that passed.

Sophia was still concerned for her, knowing that it could never really get better; one only learns to hide their emotions. She had often tried to bring Corinne to settle down once again and maybe start a family, but Corinne could never pass that line. She did not even want to speak about it, so Sophia had had no other choice but to let it go.

Now with Trent and Janessa suddenly returning to Corinne's life, Sophia only prayed that it was permanent and that Corinne did not have to face any harm or heartbreak again. She had been trying to shake off the feeling that she had been having ever since Trent's return, but it would not go away. She finally decided to sit down with Corinne and discuss her gut feeling.

"Ugh, I will call Corinne later today," Sophia muttered as she covered her ears with her pillow and shut her eyes.

Chapter Nine

Corinne flicked the sign to 'open' and went back to the counter. The door had a ringer, so she would know when someone came in. She was extra early today. She needed to be somewhere quiet that wasn't home. She went into the office and breathed in deeply. The strong smell of coffee seemed to awaken her senses and made her more alert. She smiled to herself and took a seat. Sophia would be here any minute now. She propped her legs up on the center table and reclined into her chair. She didn't hear the ringer chime or hear the door of the office opening slightly, but all of a sudden, her skin started prickling, and she felt as if someone was watching her. Her eyes popped open, and she put down her legs one after the other and then jumped from her seat like a spring.

"Hello? Anyone there?" she asked. There was no answer, so she went to the door and looked around in the café, but there was no one there. She frowned in confusion and was about to go back to her seat when the ringer chimed. She rushed to check who it was and sighed when she saw that it was Sophia.

"Hi there, Corinne."

"Hey," she said as she let out a deep breath. "It's so good to see you," she added and gave Sophia a hug. She paused to look at the door and then at the sign. She went toward it and flipped it again.

"Why are you flipping your sign to 'closed?'" Sophia asked, a little surprised.

"I have a lot of things to tell you, and I don't want people coming in yet," she answered before locking the door.

"I don't know if that would really work," Sophia said with raised eyebrows.

"Well, I still have about an hour until the shop actually opens. I have this eerie feeling someone was watching me moments ago. It almost feels like someone is stalking me." Corinne was feeling a bit awkward, not knowing how Sophia would take all of this.

"Stalking you? Why would anyone stalk you?" Sophia asked as they got into the office. Corinne sounded really surprised after hearing the question.

"I don't know. I just feel someone is stalking me." Corinne kept saying the same thing. She knew she had no explanation, but her gut feeling was screaming in her face, and she could not just get it off.

"Alright, Corinne. Let's reverse roles. What's going on?" Sophia sat at the table and looked at Corinne. She knew she had to listen.

"I have no idea. I'm as clueless as clueless can get. It feels like someone is playing mind games with me." Corinne dropped the bomb and shrugged. Sophia bit her tongue to stop herself from blurting out something that might upset Corinne.

"Well, I wouldn't know if you will find this spooky, but one strange-looking man left your shop before I came in. He left on a motorbike. Did you attend to him?" Sophia frowned.

"Spooky looking guy? I haven't seen anyone enter since I came in about fifteen minutes ago." Corinne mused. "What did he look like? Was he wearing something Halloween-ish?"

"No. he wore a rather large grey cardigan with a hood. He pulled the hood over his head as he got on his bike." Sophia widened her eyes. What if her best friend really had a stalker?

"Did you see his face?" Corinne asked, sitting up, alarmed.

"Yes, he passed just by me. He's a rather good-looking guy for someone so spooky, but seeing him still gave me the creeps." Sophia slightly shuddered.

Corinne rolled her eyes but kept on investigating. "What did he look like, Sophia?" she drawled.

"Well, he had a diamond-shaped face, almost square chin, and really black hair; even though he had them under the hood, I could still see them. I mean really black and almost shiny hair. I wondered if he poured a whole bottle of hair oil on it." Corinne furrowed her brows at the information. Frank, with the slick hair, had almost the same description.

"What kind of haircut did he have?"

Sophia looked thoughtful for a moment. "I think he had really curly hair that kept getting in his face. From what I can recall, I think he tried to pin it back with a lot of black gooey oil. But a rebellious strand refused to stay with the rest, so he has a loose curl in front of his hair." Corinne shook her head on that description, so much detail that was so much like her Sophia.

Corinne was excited, to say the least, but there was still a bit of information left. "Did he have a wart on his nose?"

Sophia looked at her and narrowed her eyes. "I think he did. He had a little wart somewhere right here." She pointed a finger just a little below the bridge of her nose. "I have this feeling like I've seen him somewhere, a déjà vu kind of feeling." Sophia looked thoughtful and tapped her cheek rhythmically.

"Was it at the party?" Corinne asked leadingly. She hoped Sophia would remember where she had seen him.

"I think so…yes! It was at your party. He had a really nice suit on and had lollipops in his pocket."

"Frank, with the slick hair!" Corinne yelled like she had hit the jackpot. She had to tell Trent.

Confused was an understatement, as Sophia looked completely lost after hearing Corinne uttering the name. "Frank with the slick hair? Who's that?"

"The creepy guy you saw today, his name is Frank, and he was at the party."

"I just told you that," Sophia stated, still confused.

"No, I mean, Janessa saw him at the party, and he gave her a lollipop."

"How sweet—"

"No, it's not sweet; the lollipop was poisoned!" Corinne gritted her teeth.

"Poisoned?"

"We believe he gave Janessa a poisoned lollipop. I woke up at midnight feeling like something was not right, and I found out she had a fever. Trent and I took her to the hospital, and the doctor said she had food poisoning. For a moment, I thought she had eaten something she had an allergy to, but she eventually mentioned this guy, and we both understood it wasn't the food. He told her he was Trent's friend, but Trent has no friend named Frank."

Sophia was stunned beyond words. "So that's why you've been on my mind. I had this feeling something was not right, but I could not just wrap my head around it. Why would anyone want to poison a child?"

"I don't have an answer to that." Corinne shrugged.

"And why is he stalking you? I'm positive that I saw him coming out of the coffee shop a few minutes ago."

"As I said, I'm as clueless as a pigeon. I have no idea who he is and why he's out to get us! I mean, Janessa could have died; goodness knows what he put in the candy. He belongs to jail."

"You need to let the police know about this." Sophia was very serious now. He could still harm Corinne and her family.

"Trent said he'd do that today," Corinne said thoughtfully. "We really need to find out who this Frank fellow is; otherwise, my brain will just explode." After a pause, she went, "Let's talk about you; how's the baby doing?"

Sophia shrugged. "She's doing fine. We all are. And Naveen has never stopped being so loving. Nikolai calls every now and then, and Frances is simply amazing. I'm surrounded by such wonderful people. And Julie calls every time she gets the chance. Mom and Dad also drop by to say hi. So, I'm perfectly good." She smiled as she mentioned the people who she loved and who adored her.

"You look like it; you're glowing. I'm glad you've found happiness." Corinne wrapped her arms around her neck. "Here, Trent is thinking of opening his own restaurant again."

"That's a lovely idea. I can't wait to see it come alive."

"Yeah, so am I. He said he stayed with some locals in Mexico, and so, he has extra things, special touches, to add to his menu."

"I'm happy he came back and that you both are back together. It's been years since I saw you blush so much." Sophia teased.

"Yeah, yeah. Rub it in," Corinne said with a grin.

"I definitely will." Sophia laughed and then cleared her throat. "Corinne, I've been trying to convince Naveen to withdraw charges against Drizella." She dropped a bomb silently.

"What? Why? After everything, she's done to you? You can't possibly expect him to give in that easily."

"Well, yes, I know she did really bad things to me and made Naveen's life very miserable, but I feel she deserves another chance. Don't you think so?" she asked in a rush.

"I don't know, girl; I don't trust that sneaky woman one bit." Corinne was now wrinkling her nose.

"Come on, Corinne. She's changed a lot; I know that."

Corinne looked at Sophia for a long moment. "Did she hex you or something? How many times have you gone to see her?"

"A couple of times," she said and looked down.

"Naveen knew about these visits?"

"Not every time."

"And did she look happy to see you?" Corinne interrogated further.

"She was surprised at first, but afterward, she was happy to see me."

"I'm 100% positive that Drizella has chameleon's DNA, she definitely isn't happy for you, and she isn't happy to see you."

"I believe she has changed, Corinne!"

"In a matter of only a few months? I wonder what wonderful formula they must be feeding them with then. I mean, she was really mean to you, Sophia. You were this close to losing your mind." Corinne gestured with the tip of her finger. "This close and you want her to roam free, so she can…I don't know, send hoodlums to throw you off a cliff and into the sea? What if you go missing this time? How will we ever find you? She won't make the same mistake of placing a call the way she did…."

"Corinne—"

"Naveen will simply die of grief and heartache."

"Corinne—"

"And your mom, oh poor Aunt Cleo. I don't want to imagine what would happen to her…."

"Corinne!" Sophia yelled. "That's enough. Nothing's going to happen to anybody. I'm not going missing, and no one is dying."

"Drizella might make sure of that!" Corinne retorted with a scoff. "She is the villain in your story, Soph, and you need to accept it for your own good and Naveen's."

"Listen to me, Corinne. You know how I am. You would think I wouldn't want her anywhere near me. But go and see her for yourself, Corinne. Drizella really has changed," Sophia said somehow imploringly. She knew Corinne could be stubborn, and Naveen was even more adamant. She thought that if she could win Corinne over, then convincing Naveen would be less of a problem.

Corinne was silent for a while. "I don't know, Sophia. As much as I want to believe you, we're talking about Drizella here. But if it makes you happy, I'll pay her a visit and let you know my thoughts."

Sophia smiled. "Thanks, Corinne." The door's ringer chimed, and they both looked at the clock; it was 8 a.m. already. Leela opened the door to the office and saw them.

"You're both here? And so early?" she asked in surprise.

"Yes, Leela, I missed the shop and my friend, so we came in earlier."

"Okay. Good. I flipped the sign; people might start coming in any moment now. I'll be in the café if you need anything."

"Sure, thanks, Leela," Corinne replied, watching her leave.

"I should be going now," Sophia said as she stood up to leave.

"Yes. I'll speak with Trent and catch up with you later," Corinne replied, also standing up.

"Alright. Corinne? Please be careful and call me if you need any help."

"I will, and you should, too. Give my regards to Naveen and Frances." They hugged each other for a long moment.

"I will. Later." Sophia waved to her friend and shut the door behind her.

Naveen was looking through the window when he finally saw Sophia driving in. He breathed a sigh of relief. She had left very early, saying she was going to the coffee shop. He had not realized until she had left, but when he had looked at the time, it was not even 7 a.m. yet. He was becoming worried, not knowing what was going on with her. He was halfway down the stairs when she came in through the door. She beamed brightly at him, and he took it as a good sign; the newly formed storm that had built inside of him was over.

"Hey there," she quipped, walking over to kiss him softly. Alright, it was a very good sign; Sophia was feeling better.

"How are you?" he asked her, breathing more easily.

"Hungry," she said, with a soft sigh that made his heart flutter.

"Frances made breakfast; I was just waiting for you."

"I can smell it already, and the aroma is so nice, my mouth is watering. I'll go find her," Sophia said and then ran to the kitchen.

Naveen watched her go and wondered what Magic had happened. Whatever it was, he was glad she was home.

He went upstairs to pick up his phone and found the table had been set for breakfast by the time he made it back into the dining room. He took his seat and studied Sophia curiously. He was going to be patient; she would eventually tell him everything. He stopped worrying and picked up his fork to enjoy the food instead.

Inspector Ryan walked down the corridor of the prison, counting until he got to the last cell. The occupant was lying on the bed and facing the wall. He wasn't sure whether she was sleeping or awake. He rapped quietly on the door, and she stirred.

"Sleeping?" he asked.

She sat up and looked at him. "Not really."

"Can we talk?" he asked softly.

"What about?" she replied, with a voice barely louder than a whisper. She looked leaner and a little pale. She had not been eating much or talking to anyone, and that made him concerned. He had had a few conversations with her these past two months, only to realize that she wished she could erase all that had happened.

"About you," he said. She raised her eyes to look at him.

"I'm not interested in talking today, Ryan."

"Just for a few minutes. It's still visiting hours, so we can talk outside."

"I don't have anything to say. Not today."

"Fine. You don't have to talk; you can just hear me out," he replied, still persisting.

She shook her head and breathed in. "Why are you concerned about me?"

"Because I have hope in you, Drizella." He unlocked the cell door and opened it. "Please, just step out and join me for a little while. Half an hour," he said, waiting for her response.

Drizella sighed and then stood up. "After you, Officer," she said with a hand gesture.

He studied her for a while and half-smiled. "I still have to lock the door," he said, waving a bunch of keys.

"Fine, do whatever you want," she said disinterestedly.

They walked at the same pace until they got to the common prison room. He pulled out a chair for her and waited for her to sit down. He sat slowly, not saying anything. The silence lingered for a while until she spoke.

"Are you talking or what?"

"Drizella, you don't have to be cranky," he said softly.

"I don't see why I am brought here, as all we are having is a moment of silence. It's nobody's funeral. Talk, or I walk," she said, with an air of finality.

He was wondering what was upsetting her so badly. "Driz, how are you doing?"

She raised her eyebrows and then rolled her eyes. "Do I have to carve it on the DPP's head before you can see that I'm fine?"

He winced at the thought of it. "I can see that you are not fine, Driz. Tell me. What's the matter?"

"What are you, my dad? I don't have to tell you anything."

"You know you can tell me everything."

"Just because we talk every once in a while doesn't mean I can tell you everything or anything at all." She lashed.

"Good. So, what's the problem?" he asked gently, seeming unfazed by her outpour.

She looked at him in a moment of brief astonishment. What kind of a fellow was he? "Did you not hear what I just said?"

"Yes, I did, and that's why I'm more interested in what's going on with you. What's running through that head of yours? You are not eating; you are not talking to anybody. What's the matter?" He poured.

"Do you really want to know what the matter is?" she asked in a low and deadly tone. "Fine, then I'll tell you. I'm tired. I'm sick and tired of this place. I want out of here. Be somewhere far away, where nobody knows me. I want a breath of clean, fresh air and a chance to start life anew. That's what is wrong. I have no friends, no family, no place to call my own, I have nothing," she said, throwing up her hand for emphasis.

Ryan looked at her, speechless. "Wow," he said at last. "I didn't know you were going through all that."

"Like it would solve anything," she scoffed. "And don't you go around telling me to plead guilty in court. I don't want to hear that bullshit. Whether I plead guilty or not, the least I'm spending here is ten years," she said, with masked sadness.

"You might not have to if we can convince Mr. Hawk to withdraw his charges against you."

She almost laughed. "Naveen? Withdraw his charges? I don't think so. It would be easier to teach an elephant yoga than to make him change his mind. He won't. Not in a million years," she said, in a tone that showed she was sure of what she was saying.

"I think it can be possible." He repeated again.

"Arrogant. Inspector, you are very arrogant. What makes you so confident? Have you two become friends overnight? Even Rick couldn't convince him. Who do you think you are? A voodoo man with tricks up his sleeve? Are you going to, I don't know, swing a stopwatch in front of his eyes and hypnotize him? You make me laugh," she said, taking a more relaxed position in her chair.

He snickered at her sense of humor. "Magic. Hmm, that could work? I know someone who could help you."

Drizella frowned in confusion and sat up. "What are you saying?"

He cleared his throat and leaned forward. "I have been speaking with Sophia."

"And?" She suddenly became interested in the possibility.

"She promised to speak with him," he replied. "So, we can be hopeful."

"I don't know, inspector. Naveen can be as stubborn as a mule," she drawled thoughtfully. "But if Sophia really is willing to help, then perhaps it might be possible," she said finally. She really hoped it would be possible then. If Sophia was involved, luck could be on her side. She would at least get a chance to apologize sincerely and then disappear from their lives forever.

"I see the two of you have become very good friends." Ryan noted.

"To my surprise, inspector. To my surprise," she said with a little smile. "She really is a wonderful person. I see why Naveen loves her so much. I'm happy for him. Anyways, whatever it is, I don't want to get my hopes up too high."

"I understand. Keep your fingers crossed for the best."

Drizella smiled and shrugged a little. "Not so sure I can do that, but I will try. As far as I'm concerned, Naveen wants my head on a silver platter."

"You will be fine, Drizella. I know you will," Ryan added, with a calm look on his face and a smile that lit hope in Drizella's heart.

Would Sophia really do this? She didn't know. She could only hope, and hope was a strange and new word she was willing to embrace.

Sophia had had strange dreams those days, to the point where she thought she was going paranoid. Naveen had also assured her that there was nothing she should be afraid of because they were together. Sophia then had stopped talking about these dreams she was having, as she thought he would become even more paranoid than she was. She only wanted him to be happy.

Most nights, after a bad dream would awaken her, she'd quietly sit in her bed and stare at Naveen's perfect face, which looked so calm and serene when he was in a deep slumber. She sometimes felt that their life was turning into a movie, hers and Corinne's, with a thrill coming up every once in a while. They even had had a good laugh about it when she had shared those thoughts with Corinne.

Corinne had gone like: "I just hope there is no more drama or suspense now. I've had enough of it, I swear." Sophia could not agree more. She just wanted some peace, like real peace, as she was surrounded by people who loved her; no more Drizellas or anyone else.

Little did she know, there was a lot more coming in for her and her best friend. A new tempest was waiting for them.

Chapter Ten

Trent had lodged a complaint at the police department about the man who had been stalking his wife and had allegedly poisoned his daughter. When he gave descriptions of the person to the cops, they had called for a sketch artist to draw the face described by Trent. He called Corinne and asked her to bring Janessa to the station since she was the one who had the most seen the man. Corinne arrived shortly with both Janessa and Sophia. The sketch artist looked up at the three ladies and then at Trent.

"Did they all see him?" he asked, somewhat befuddled.

"They both did, except her," Trent replied, pointing toward Corinne.

"Well, that will make it a lot easier if they both saw the same fellow." He pulled his pencil from behind his ear, where he had tucked it, and flipped his sketch pad open to a new sheet.

"Wait," Sophia said suddenly. "Can you back up the sheets a little bit?" She said, frowning with her eyes still glued to his drawing pad.

"Alright," He flipped three pages back, and she told him to stop, waving her hand frantically, her eyes lingering to the sheet of paper, slipping onto the features of a man drawn on the sheet.

"Who is this man?" she asked with wide eyes.

"Oh, just some random fellow a woman described some days ago. She said she had been seeing him prowl around the neighborhood at Crossbow Avenue time and time again. She thought he looked suspicious and had decided to report him. He looks really creepy, always dressed in an oversized grey cardigan and with hair as black as a crow's feathers. Would you happen to recognize him? The police are looking for him already," he added, flipping the sheets back, ready to start sketching again.

"Yes!" Janessa called out. "This man looks like him." She took a deep look at the sketch artist and then at Trent and Sophia, who nodded as their eyes met.

The sketch artist was suddenly getting impatient. This was not an art gallery with an exhibition going on. He rolled his eyes and twirled the pencil he had in his hand. "Listen, little princess, how 'bout we take you and your aunt's description and see if it matches the man we have here already?" He hit the sketchbook with his pencil and went on with a forced smile. She nodded. "Good. Now be a good girl and tell me what the man with the candies looked like and what he was wearing? Try to remember everything, all the tiny details, okay? Did he have any tattoos or funny-looking shoes or umbrella ears?" He was joking to make Janessa comfortable so she could describe the man more easily.

"No, silly, he's a human, not a cartoon character."
Janessa was covering her mouth with her little hand as she
giggled and went on to describe him.

The sketch artist was only halfway done when he
realized that they were both right. The man in the previous
portrait was the same as the one they were currently
sketching. He frowned as he continued to sketch. He finally
sighed and looked at Sophia when he was done. "I have to
admit; you have great eyesight." He raised the sketch up for
them to see. "Is this him?" he asked.

Sophia looked at the picture with scrutiny;
something was still missing that she could not quite put the
finger on. The resemblance was uncanny, but something
was left out of the picture. "I don't know for sure, but it
looks like it is him but not him at the same time. Can you
sketch another one? I think there is a detail we have missed
out." She gave a full description of his face, while this time,
the sketch was made in black and white.

"Frank Hamish." Someone had said out loud behind them when the artist was done. They all turned back, slightly startled.

The cop who had just spoken looked at them all as they stared at him. He had a paper cup in his hand and gestured toward the portrait. "Frank Hamish, that's his name. He's the one bothering you, mam?" he asked Sophia, who looked at the others in utter confusion.

"Yes. Do you know him?" Trent asked.

"Through investigations. He is on our top ten wanted criminal list here. Slippery as an eel. But why is he after you? Have you been in a brawl with him or something?" The officer looked skeptical. The people in front of him did not look like the lot that will mess with someone like Frank Hamish; he was big fish.

"No, I don't even know him!" Trent said in a defensive voice. Why would he have anything to do with a criminal, after all?

"You are sure about that? Hamish here doesn't stalk people or mark them as prey unless he wants a pound of flesh. We have gathered that over the years. Think about it, Mr...?"

"Martinez. Trent Martinez." Trent extended his hand to shake the cop's.

The cop shifted in surprise and faced him entirely as he took his hand, "Trent Martinez? The same Martinez who won the Hot Plate cooking contest three years ago?"

"Yes, I am the same guy." Trent forced a smile while his stomach was filled with crazy butterflies. Fear crept on him as it hit him that a dangerous man, a criminal, stalked his family. What do they do now? He had almost killed their baby girl; why? Trent had so many questions creating havoc inside his head, which he needed urgent answers to.

"My, my, my," the cop said in a loud voice, slapping the sketch artist's back. "Jason, why didn't you tell me I was standing before royalty? That contest was crazy. Man, am I glad to see you! I'm a huge fan! Can I get an autograph?" he asked, excited like a teenager suddenly. His request was met with silence and a pair of eyes staring at him. "Okay then, no autographs. But you need to find out why this guy is after you. Try to remember where you have met him. As far as I know, he only wants you for one thing, and that's revenge." He scratched his head.

"But I don't know him!" Trent said with a frustrated tone.

"Apparently, he knows you. There's no other explanation. When you have it figured out, get back to us. Until then, we might have to put a tracking device on you in particular, in case you go missing."

The sketch artist nodded. "We might have to put it on all of them. Any one of them could go missing." He was chewing the back of his pencil, looking at them.

Corinne looked disturbed at the piece of dangerous information. "But we don't even know this guy," she said helplessly. "What if he tries to harm us again?"

The cop shook his head. "I think you do, but you probably don't remember him. If not you, then Mr. Martinez must know him from somewhere. And until you are able to remember it all, we have to make sure we can track your every move so as to find him easily. As far as I know, he'll be back, and soon." The cop left the words hanging ominously.

"Not helping," the sketch artist whispered at the cop as he took in the scared faces of Trent, Corinne, and Sophia one by one.

Corinne rubbed her temples furiously as she glanced in Sophia's direction, looking extremely exhausted instantly. "I am going to lose my mind if it keeps going like this, Sophia." Sophia's heart went out to her sister-like friend who had always been so strong, and now when things had finally started getting better for her, a new pandora box had been opened out of nowhere.

"Tell me about it," Sophia replied glumly as she extended an arm and hugged her.

"I wish to heaven that I knew what was going on," Corinne said, as Sophia rubbed her shoulder soothingly.

"You need to stay calm, though," Sophia said with a smile while patting Corinne's shoulder.

"Isn't this amazing? Staying calm used to be so easy until this thug showed up. I have never been more scared, ever." Corinne shut her eyes tightly as if she was in the middle of a nightmare, and she was waiting for it to be over.

"Nothing's going to happen, Corinne." Sophia tried to smile reassuringly, but she could tell that she was not convincing enough.

"Girl, right now, I wish I could believe that. I really wish I could. But right now, all I can hear is the ache in my head and the hungry rumblings of my stomach." Corinne sat up and tapped Janessa gently on the head. She looked up from the tablet she had been playing a game on. "You hungry, baby?"

"Yes, I am." Janessa nodded and adorably patted her tummy. They all smiled at her.

"Should we go out for lunch or just go home and order in? I think the order sounds safer."

"Don't be paranoid, Corinne." Trent rolled his eyes, even though he was shit scared too.

"I'm not being paranoid; I am just being safe. Who knows, he might be lurking around the corner. I don't know about you, but I don't want to be someone's lunch." She was shuddering delicately while picking up her phone.

"Someone's lunch? That is the most ridiculous thing ever." Sophia laughed. "What is he, a vampire?"

"No, a crocodile," piped Trent.

"A dinosaur," chimed Janessa, and they all laughed out loud. The sun seemed to come out of the cloud for a second.

"You can't be too careful," Corinne replied with a smile.

Trent was pacing up and down his study. He had looked at the picture over a thousand times, but nothing seemed to click or light up. He was as blank as trying to remember someone he had never met. He sat heavily in his swivel chair, exhausted. He didn't realize it when his eyes closed slowly, and soon he was fast asleep in a sitting position.

Several houses down the street, in a dimly lit basement with pictures held to a board with thumbtacks and pushpins, Frank Hamish was plotting his next move. He had marked several pictures with an X and had thrown a dart at Trent's picture. He took a framed photo out of a drawer and held it up to the light.

"Just a little longer, Father, just a little longer, and I'll avenge your death. The man who caused your death is back in town, and I will make sure I get your revenge for you. It's my promise, and I'll keep it." He was muttering to himself solemnly. The only thing on his mind was revenge.

Naveen took a while to process all the information. He wondered what cloud loomed over them. Maybe history was replaying itself; he started thinking deeply. "Hamish is danger walking on two legs," he said finally.

"How do you know?" Sophia asked him, startled.

"He has always been. If you take his shoe, he takes your house. I knew his father and his brother. They were a dangerous lot. I have known them since I was in High school. It is a long story that I haven't told anyone," he said with a distant sigh. "I have not thought about it in years, sixteen to be precise."

"Can you now tell me?" Sophia asked silently. "Only if you want to." She stammered at last as he looked at her, and Naveen smiled lovingly, nodding his head.

"Yes. I think I can now." He mused reflectively. "Frances knows the story, given she has been our housekeeper since forever. My mom died when I was three, so Frances literally raised my brother and me together with our dad. My dad was a realtor, and he made sure my brother Scott and I had everything we ever needed. My dad and Nelson Hamish were good friends, that is until he began losing clients to my dad."

"So, what happened?" Sophia was biting her lip; she was listening to him intently.

"He decided to take my dad off the scene. Tampered with his car brakes so it would look like an accident, but everyone knew it was not. The hostility was all too obvious before the staged accident happened. Unfortunately, it was not just my dad that was in the car that 5th of June; Scott was with him too." He reflected grimly. Sophia's heart dropped in the pits of her stomach.

"Oh, my. They both died?" She covered her mouth with her hand.

"My dad did on the spot. My brother did hours later." Naveen pulled a thread out of his sleeve, looking down. Sophia thought it was an attempt to hide the pain in his eyes.

"Oh, Naveen. I'm so sorry," Sophia said after a brief silence. She then stood up and walked to him. Naveen looked up, and there it was, the pain he had been hiding for years. Sophia's heart melted as she wrapped her arms around him. He was sitting while Sophia stood, so Naveen could lay his head on her belly as she ran her fingers in his hair. "I am so sorry." She kissed him on the head. "I know this won't change things, but you are not alone, Naveen. Stop hiding under the blanket of pain, please." She begged.

"It's been over sixteen years now. I could not do anything then, I was too scared, and I was too young. But I was shattered. Scott was my hero; I really looked up to him. And my dad was everything a father should be." He looked up and smiled with his eyes wet.

"What happened afterward?"

Naveen shrugged. "I could not prove that he did it. So, I decided to build myself and to build my empire. Rick was my only friend from childhood, so he understood me a lot, and Frances was there all the way."

"Is that why you have never mentioned them?" Sophia asked softly.

"I would have told you eventually. But with Hamish on the scene, Trent needs to be extra careful. That man can't be trusted." Naveen started shaking his head. He could not let Hamish harm any of the people he loved or cared about again.

"The cops are in on it already." Sophia assured him.

"The cops will need double hands to catch him. It's not going to be easy. The sooner they track him down, the better. He is not an easy target. Never been one."

"I'm worried now." As Sophia shivered a little, Naveen pressed her body closer to his.

"So am I, but I will take care of you, love," Naveen replied. There was a long silence in the room, and after a while, he felt there was something else she wanted to say. "Sophia, you want to tell me something else?" he asked, raising his head again from her belly.

"No, it's nothing," she said hurriedly. However, the way she spoke gave it all away; there was something up with her for sure.

Amused, he smiled a little, stood up, and went over to her side. He took her hand and brought her to the couch, where he made her sit down before he sat beside her and playfully tugged at her ear. "Your eyelid is twitching, Sophia. Tell me. What is it? Is it about Hamish?"

"No. It's not him. It's...it's someone else." Sophia shut her eyes and clutched his hand, gently looking extremely cute.

"Someone bothering you?" he asked, his voice laced with apprehension. "Tell me, Sophia, please." There was a plea in his voice. Each time he felt her acting this way, he feared that he might lose her again, which he would never want to. Losing Sophia would be like losing his own self in a dark alley, where there was no oxygen.

"No, it's not that. No one is bothering me. Perhaps we should talk about it some other time. I don't want to upset you any more than you already are." Sophia sighed and patted her tummy lightly; the baby would sometimes move in her belly now.

"Is it Drizella?" he asked, with a smile that said he knew already.

"How did you…? Did I mention her name by mistake?" She was sure she had not, or had she?

"It is her then." He nodded slowly.

"Naveen—" Sophia began.

"Sophia. We have talked about this before, and I said no." He watched her countenance fall, and he felt his heart squeeze, but Naveen knew it was for her own good, for their good.

"I understand," she said, silently drawing a pattern on her thigh with the tip of her index finger.

"But I thought about it." Naveen continued. She was now looking up at him. "And I think you are right. She does deserve another chance. I spoke with the inspector, and he told me the same thing you have been saying. So, I won't be pressing charges against her anymore," he said with a gentle smile.

She beamed at him, her face glowing, "Oh, Naveen. Thank you. Honestly, I can't wait to see her out of there. Thank you again." She turned toward him and hugged him hard.

"Hey, can't breathe." He laughed and then went on, "I am doing this for you. Just for you," he said, kissing the top of her head. "I will complete all the necessary formalities tomorrow."

"Thank you, Naveen. I love you," Sofia said with a contented sigh. For a brief moment, they forgot about Hamish. But again, only briefly, as the danger was much nearer than they were realizing.

Naveen's body was twitching, and his face was contorted with pain. He mombled something while rolling to his side, looking very uncomfortable even in his sleep. Sophia had woken up to go to the bathroom, and when she had returned, she could tell that Naveen was having a nightmare. She had seen him having those episodes earlier as well. When she had asked him, he would always say it was nothing. Sophia knew now what that was all about.

Sophia sighed and switched on the table lamp, filling the room with a soft caramel color light. Naveen stirred and mombled something again. He looked like he was having a terrible nightmare. Sophia felt an urge to wake him up and end the suffering. She was twisting her fingers and biting her lip, not sure what to do.

"Naveen?" she softly called his name as he was stirring in the bed again. Her voice trembled, but then she took two steps further and bent over him. "Nav, love. Are you okay?" She gently shook his arm, being extra careful not to scare him any more than he already looked.

"Scott, no. Please stay. I will be so alone. No!" Naveen's voice was merely a whisper, but Sophia felt as if he was a little kid, scared and lonely. She wanted to hold him while she sang to him and rocked back and forth until all his fears are gone. She wanted him to know that he was loved and protected.

For the world, he might be the strong man who set his own empire, the phoenix who had risen up out of the ashes, but now that she had seen his wounds, still not healed properly, she felt for him. For a moment, she regretted breaking his heart when she did. He was in desperate need of love so that he could heal himself. She felt like loving him, be there for him.

She gently touched his face with her fingers, her hand slightly shaking. Some tears rolled down on her cheek; she was crying for the man she loved—the man who had been through hell alone and came back more affectionate than ever. He had never let the darkness consume him; he was her hero.

He had told her that his brother was his own hero, but she wanted to wake him up and tell him that he was her hero.

"Tomorrow, I shall tell him tomorrow." Sophia smiled to herself and planted a kiss on Naveen's forehead before switching off the light and getting back in bed again. She turned toward him and hugged him from behind. He had to know that he was protected, too. In a low but soothing voice, Sophia began singing to him. Naveen shifted a little, but then his breathing became slower as her voice pushed him into a deeper and peaceful sleep. The pain on his face faded ever so slowly, and he relaxed in her arms. Sophia kept humming under her breath;

> The heart is a bloom
>
> Shoots up through the stony ground
>
> There's no room
>
> No space to rent in this town

You're out of luck

And the reason that you had to care

The traffic is stuck

And you're not moving anywhere

  You thought you'd found a friend

  To take you out of this place

  Someone you could lend a hand

  In return for grace

It's a beautiful day

Sky falls, you feel like

It's a beautiful day

Don't let it get away

  You're on the road

  But you've got no destination

  You're in the mud

  In the maze of her imagination

You're lovin' this town

Even if that doesn't ring true

You've been all over

And it's been all over you

  It's a beautiful day

Don't let it get away

It's a beautiful day

Touch me

Take me to that other place

Teach me

I know I'm not a hopeless case

See the world in green and blue

See China right in front of you

See the canyons broken by cloud

See the tuna fleets clearing the sea out

See the Bedouin fires at night

See the oil fields at first light and

See the bird with a leaf in her mouth

After the flood, all the colors came out

It was a beautiful day

Don't let it get away

Beautiful day

Touch me

Take me to that other place

Reach me

I know I'm not a hopeless case

What you don't have, you don't need it now

What you don't know you can feel it somehow

What you don't have, you don't need it now

Don't need it now

It was a beautiful day

Chapter Eleven

Trent got out of his car and locked the doors before turning around to look at the outer part of the building that had once been his restaurant. He had been known for his gourmet cooking all over the city. Such fame made critics want to come over, which pressured him to maintain the restaurant's culinary presence. He smiled to himself as he remembered the bittersweet experience that came with their visits.

Once, a critic was disappointed, only because the food contained onions that prima donna was allergic to. He had then noted the potential loop and took proper precautions to avoid other food allergy complaints. Each step he was taking on the property was bringing back delicious moments from his memory: the most recent of them being when he had been invited for a cooking contest where he literally knocked out the other opponents. For a moment then, he thought he might not be up to it, but with every gourmet chef falling with each round, he ended up winning the competition. He won by a narrow margin, but he still won.

He couldn't remember which chef lost to him in the final, but he remembered the fellow was not very happy. Sometimes he wished he had not won the competition. Winning took him to an all-expense paid sea trip as part of the reward, but the ship he was on was wrecked, and he almost lost his life, as well as his daughter's. Due to a strange series of events, he disappeared and lost contact with his wife for the following three years.

He opened the door of the restaurant and met his assistant, who was already waiting for him. "Jean Dubois," he said, greeting the assistant with a bright smile.

"Trent Martinez!" The reply came with a burst of hearty laughter. "It's nice to see you again, old friend. We thought we had lost you," he said in a heavy French accent, slapping him playfully on the back.

"I am a survivor." Trent grinned.

"Am I glad to see you? When you called, saying you were back in town, I did a jig and dusted out my ol' chef's cap. We are back in business, oui?"

"Absolutely, Dubois, absolutely." Trent beamed.

"And I'm sure you must have new ideas for a more classic upgrade, oui?"

"Well, I'd say we can do the brainstorming together. What do you think?" Trent replied, scratching his chin. He was sure that Dubois would come up with something wonderful as usual. His mind was always bursting with exciting ideas.

Jean Dubois rubbed his hands in pure delight; his eyes were bright as lamps. "I've been thinking of a revamp. Let's bring the beach to the people. Hawaiian style, with a twist of urban high life, burgers, and burritos. A little bit of the countryside, theme Texas."

Trent shook his head in disbelief. "It is a restaurant, Chef Dubois. Not a fiesta."

"Exactly! Fiesta style...." Dubois went on excitedly, talking about things that made Trent laugh until his sides began to ache.

"Alright, alright. I think we'll stick to the chandelier and the furniture revamp. Not the fiesta."

"But...oh come on, you can't possibly not want a fiesta; everybody likes good food and colors!" Dubois protested.

"Sorry, Dubois, no fiesta. I will put a call through to Maxi. He can help with that," he said.

"Maxi? I haven't heard from him in a long time. He might have left the country," he added, taking a last look around the restaurant. "This place is going to be ship-shape in no time, *mon ami*. I eagerly await the smell of cooking in my nostrils once again. The taste of beautiful French wine. I can hear the sizzle already." He piqued in excitement. "You give my best regards to your wife, Martinez. I'll be sending her some scallops very soon, the best one from the gourmet market," he said excitedly. "Oh, it feels good to be back."

"I trust your instincts; she would like that very much. Thanks a lot, Chef Dubois; see you tomorrow." Trent waved to his French partner and turned on his heels to leave the restaurant.

"Anything for an old friend. *Au revoir*," Dubois said and headed for the light switches.

Trent started his car, with some of Dubois's excitement rubbing off on him. His next stop was supposed to be the police department to determine how far the investigation had gone, but he decided to check on Corinne instead. He would go to the police department afterward. Trent drummed merrily on the steering wheel, driving at a steady pace. As he looked ahead and saw the traffic light switch from green to yellow, he pressed hard on the accelerator, hoping to beat the light before it turned red. He watched the needle go up and, for a fleet moment, did not see the oversized truck that came out of the right turn just a few meters ahead. He slammed on the brakes, but they did not budge.

"What?" He tried and tried, only to realize they weren't working. If they eventually did work, he didn't notice it, as the airbag inflated and the lights went out.

Corinne was looking at her watch; she had lost count of how many times she had turned her wrist to check what time it was.

"He said he would be here in ten minutes, and that was about two hours ago! Why isn't he here yet?" she asked to no one in particular. She was pacing up and down the office in leveled apprehension. "Stay calm, Corinne. He will be here at any moment. Stay calm and remain positive," she was telling herself. The breathing therapy did not work, no matter how hard she tried. She simply could not erase the feeling that something was terribly wrong. This sinking feeling had now become a permanent part of her.

"Three cappuccinos, please. All decaf," someone said from outside the café. The voice was familiar, so she rushed to the door.

"Sophia!" she yelled. "Thank goodness you're here!"

"What's the matter?" Sophia asked, perplexed as she looked at Corinne's paling face.

"Trent called about two hours ago, saying he'd be here in ten minutes, ten minutes! But he hasn't shown up. His line is not reachable either, and I have a strong feeling he's in trouble," she explained, without even stopping to breathe.

"I saw daddy's car on the way here," Janessa quipped innocently; Sophia had taken Janessa out.

"Where? Where did you see it?" Corinne bent to sit on her knees in front of her little daughter while her heart sank in the pits of her stomach.

"In front of the book store. It looked smashed in the fender and the glass, too," the little girl told them, now looking scared and somehow realizing what might have happened to her father.

Corinne looked like she was going to pass out. "Accident? Was Trent involved in an accident? I can't believe it. This can't be. I can't believe it." She sunk heavily into her chair, with her hands to her face.

"Janessa, did you notice anything else? Any ambulance? Any other cars?" Sophia asked her, hoping she had seen some other car. She herself did not.

"Nope." Janessa was shaking her little head. "Our car was moving a bit too fast, and I could not really look. But I don't think I saw him in the car."

"Oh, dear. What are we going to do? Where could he be by now?" Corinne lamented.

Not knowing what exactly to say, Sophia started, "We could go to the—"

"Hospital! We could go to the hospital and check. We could ask them if he's been brought there." Corinne stood up as if in a state of a dream and looked around for her handbag. "Where is that bag? Where is it?"

"It's right in front of you, Corinne. Let off some steam. You need to stay calm," Sophia said, and Corinne stared at her as though she were invisible.

"Fine, I'll stay calm. I'm calm. See? I'm perfectly fine. Right. So, can we leave now?" Corinne's voice shook, and she felt a huge lump rising in her throat.

"Trent will be fine, Corinne," Sophia said calmly, hoping the words would register. She had never seen Corinne so disorientated and frazzled. It was strange seeing this side of her best friend; she wished she could fix all of her problems at once. Corinne gave her an empty stare. "Trent will be fine," Sophia reassured her. "Trust me. We will find him, and he will be fine." Corinne nodded and sighed deeply. Sophia could see the tension evaporate a little, but it was too thick to lift so easily. She knew seeing Trent alive, and well was all that could lift it. She hoped he was fine as they got into her car and headed for the city hospital.

Corinne sat on the stairs outside the hospital. Helpless could not begin to define her look. Sophia sighed and held her by the shoulders. "Corinne...."

"He is not here either, Sophia. He is not in any of the hospitals. Where do you think he could be?" Corinne grabbed her hair in her fists and pulled them slightly; that was how frustrated she was.

"I don't know, Corinne. I don't have an answer for you. We got to file a missing person report." Sophia suggested.

"How is that going to help?" she replied, getting close to tears.

"Daddy has a tracking device on him. The policeman said they'd put one on him, remember?" Janessa reminded them. She was such a smart kid.

Corinne pulled Janessa in a tight embrace. "How could I forget about that! I am so glad I have you, sweetheart." That piece of information gave Corinne hope.

"We should leave now," Sophia said.

"Yes, I hope we are not too late." Corinne ran her hand in her hair, trying to pull herself together.

"Think positive thoughts, Corinne."

"I'm trying, Sophia. I'm trying. It's just not working," she replied in a helpless tone.

"At least we know how to find him, so cheer up. Come on, let's go find Trent." Sophia took her hand and gave it an assuring squeeze.

Trent was fighting to keep his eyes open. His vision was blurry, and his head sounded like a train's whistle. He was wrestling against heavy sleepiness that was beclouding him as he was trying to recognize his surroundings. Dimly lit, it was nowhere familiar to him. He could hear the soft whirring of a fan and the sound of someone clicking away at a computer's keyboard. He tried to talk, but no sound left his lips. He tried again, and this time his voice sounded muffled; only then did he realize he had been duct-taped. He made louder, muffled noises and struggled to move, but the ropes that held him tied to a chair would not budge. He moved again and again until the chair made a scraping sound on the floor. He stopped then, and the clicking on the keyboard stopped as well. There was silence for a while until someone harshly and swiftly pulled the duct tape from his mouth. He growled in sudden pain and looked up at the hooded face staring at him.

"Who the hell are you?" he rasped in anger.

"The grim reaper," came the dry reply.

Trent rolled his eyes. "Yeah, right. And I'm the dream catcher. Who are you, and what do you want with me? Why have you brought me here? And what is this place, a basement?"

"Easy there, Martinez. One question at a time. Be a good schoolboy and ask one question at a time," the goon said, patting Trent on the head like a little boy.

Irritated, Trent snapped. "You better tell me who you are and what you want, else you'll be sorry."

"Tell me something I don't know, Martinez," the hood replied, slowly walking around him as he spoke. "You are injured, can't move, and tied to a chair. Tell me, what can you do? Nothing!" He taunted, coming to a halt in front of him and bending, so he could look at him directly in the eye. "You, my friend, can do nothing. You know why? You are stuck. With me. At my mercy. You are helpless, Martinez, helpless!"

The attack was swift, and he hadn't seen it coming. The goon felt the impact of the head butt on his nose before he could see it. He held his nose and groaned in agony. He staggered to the light switch and flicked it on. His hand came away with blood. He looked at Trent with a fresh wave of anger and took measured steps toward him.

"You dare to hit me, Martinez. You struck the first blow. You wait and see what I do to you."

"Go to hell!" Trent retorted.

The man pulled back his hood to reveal his face. "Remember me?" he said, with a sinister smile that revealed a set of perfect dentitions.

Trent was beyond words. This was the man in the sketch live right in from of him. "You. Frank…Frank Hamish," he stuttered.

"The one and only," Hamish replied, with a pseudo tip of the hat act. "It's a pleasure meeting the Famous Trent Martinez in person. Once again." His voice was cool, a sign of imminent danger. Apprehension built up within Trent, but he stayed still.

"What do you mean?" he asked.

"You really can't remember? Think, Martinez. Six years ago, a man with the name Nelson Hamish. Ring a bell?"

Nelson Hamish. It sounded familiar but not too much as to light up a bulb.

"Think, gourmet chef. Six months after, you had had a critic complaining of onion allergies. You served a man mussels and Brussels sprouts soup. Think. Try to remember."

Trent closed his eyes. It was all he could do to keep himself from rolling his eyes. Thousands of people had been served mussels and Brussels sprouts soup in his restaurant. It would be ridiculous to think he could remember one person who was neither a friend nor a regular. He shook his head. "Nothing!" He shrugged.

Hamish's eyes darkened at his response. "You seem to have a short-term memory, I see. The most asked item on your menu that year killed my father. Your restaurant served him mussels that had goodness knows what, and that led to his death. You killed Nelson Hamish! You killed my father!"

"That is not true. That cannot be possible. We didn't serve and still do not serve food to the detriment of people's health."

"Pompous Chef Martinez. Of course, why would you? You own a five-star restaurant; you think you can make no mistakes."

"We try not to make mistakes. We are not claiming to be perfect." Trent acknowledged.

Hamish walked over to a drawer and brought out a pistol slowly. "I could have forgiven you based on what you just said, Martinez. My, my, you really can come up with a good defense," he said, turning swiftly toward him with the gun in his hand, making Trent's heart jump. "But I can't forgive you. You know why? I keep promises. I promised my father, and myself, and my brother that whenever I set my eyes on you, I'd make sure to get even. Do you remember my brother? Dale Hamish." He smirked.

Trent frowned; once again, the name rang a bell, faintly, maybe a flickering bulb.

"Hot Plate," Hamish said with a dark frown.

Trent tried hard to remember what Dale Hamish had to do with the Hot Plate Contest.

"He was a contestant as well as you three years ago. My brother owned a restaurant that had everybody's health and allergies in mind. He was a healthy eating advocate, no junk, no calories, low cholesterol. But you, you were all of that. Everything allergies."

Trent gritted his teeth. Hamish was beginning to grate on his nerves. He had a passionate hatred for false allegations, much less anything that included life. He was beginning to seethe as Hamish went on and on like a windbag.

"My brother lost to you in that contest. He was just two points from winning, and you made him lose. And that too with what?"

"Mussels and Brussels sprout soup." Trent remembered. It all made sense now. He remembered Dale Hamish, even though Nelson Hamish still sounded like a myth to him. He understood now why Frank Hamish was all out to get him. He had been unlucky to get tangled with his entire family. It was pure bad luck, nothing more and nothing less. If he did survive this encounter with Frank Hamish, he would make sure to get his stars checked and avoid anyone with the name Hamish for the rest of his life. If he survived, that is.

"Smart brains, Martinez. Smart brains." He clapped, jolting him out of his reverie. "Now, you remember. The very soup that killed my father sent my brother out of business. The grief ruined him forever. If he had lost to someone else, I would have felt fine with it, but he lost to you, and losing is not something we know how to handle well in the family. We either win, or no one does. You should have just stayed in the ocean when you were shipwrecked. For a moment, I thought nature fought on my behalf, but you survived, and you came back. So, I decided I was going to pay you a visit, old friend." His smile was sinister and sent cold chills into Trent's bones. He wished somehow the police would find them before this deranged lunatic who was bent on revenge killed him.

Trent's mind was about to explode. The situation was dangerously difficult yet funny at the same time. How could he mess with people like these without even realizing it? How could a man blame Trent for doing him wrong only by feeding soup to a client and winning a competition? It was cynical.

"Is that why you poisoned my daughter?

"Oh, that was just the tip of the iceberg. It was just to rattle you a little. A teeny-weenie warm up to flex my fingers. She was lucky you saved her. I'll see how much of that you can do when you are dead."

"Stay away from my family, Frank Hamish!" Trent growled.

"Oh, but I won't. We have to get even, don't you think? I'll kill you right here. Then go send your wife out of business. Now that sounds like fun." He was smirking, looking like a crazy guy.

"I did not kill your dad, Frank. I did not cheat your brother either. You have gotten it all twisted." Trent shut his eyes and emphasized each word. What was even going on inside Hamish's head? It could not be real.

"No, you are the one who has gotten it all twisted. But anyway, what does it matter? You can just begin to say your last prayers." He tightened his hand on the pistol grip and cocked the gun, ready to fire. Fear crept upon Trent; he did not want to die like that, away from his family.

"Listen, you really don't have to do this. We can talk this over…." Trent added, trying to persuade him.

"Quiet," Hamish replied while firing into the air. "There will be no more talking or the next bullet...." He cocked the gun again. "Goes into your head. Which it will eventually. Only sooner. This face, Martinez, is the last face you will ever see." He aimed at Trent's head and watched him close his eyes.

Trent then heard shots. The door burst open just as the gun went off twice and then one more time. An excruciating pain shot through his chest. The shock knocked him out even before the impact of the bullet did. He felt the chair topple backward before darkness wrapped him in a cold and welcoming embrace, but not before he heard someone call his name.

"Trent!"

"Corinne," he whispered, and then he bowed to darkness.

He found himself in a dark alley with countless mahogany doors filling the corridor on both sides. The place was so dimly lit that he could not guess the length of the alley at first. He hesitantly took a step forward, making sure not to trip on something.

"Hello?" he called out, his voice echoing in the narrow alley sounding even weird to his own ears. There was no answer as he kept walking forward. The doors looked exactly alike, so nobody could tell which one led out of the dark alley. There was a strange stench in the air, which was making it difficult to breathe. He opened his mouth to fill his lungs with some air, and that was when a sharp stab of pain pierced his chest cavity.

"Ow," he yelped, and reflexively, his hand reached for the point where the pain had hit. He felt something sticky and warm oozing out of the wound. It was dark but not enough to know that it was blood. Suddenly, it hit him that the whole place reeked of blood. An uneasy feeling rose inside his stomach, which brought him back to his senses. The exit? He had to find the exit and leave that place soon.

"Trent?" Someone was calling his name. He turned around in desperation and started looking for the source of the voice but failed miserably. "Trent, look at me?" The voice insisted, and his eyes lingered to one of the doors at the very end, which was a part of the dark alley but still shone like a neon sign. It was his door, the place where the source of the voice was, his life, Corinne.

Trent rushed to the door when he heard her again, "Is he going to be okay?" She was crying, which was kind of funny because Corinne hardly ever cried. They always joked that she would not even cry at Trent's funeral. He wanted to yell at her that he was not dead yet and that she should not cry, but was he really alive?

He tried to say something, but his voice wouldn't reach her. He was now by the door, and before he could turn the knob, he heard someone calling his name again, but it was not Corinne. He once again turned to look who it was, and in the middle of the dark alley, it was Hamish.

"Ugh, not again!" Trent groaned, and a venomous smile spread across Hamish's face that made him look scary in the half-darkness.

"I am coming to get you, Martinez," Hamish whispered, and the whisper echoed in the alley, too.

"Not this time, sucker," Trent said before turning the knob.

"Trent? Oh my God, he is bleeding." Corinne shrieked and shook his shoulder. Trent's eyes were shut, and fresh blood was oozing out of the wound in his chest. There were loud noises of scraping metal and approaching footsteps before a team of paramedics entered the basement.

Someone took her hand softly and tried to pull her back, but Corinne wouldn't budge. Her other hand was gently tapping Trent's cheek, trying to bring him back, but his skin under her touch was going colder, and it was scaring her.

"Mam, please back off; we need to check on him," a paramedic said as his team rushed to attend to Trent.

Sophia grabbed her hand once again and went on, "Corinne, Trent needs medical attention. He will be just fine."

Corinne nodded and took a few steps back, but her eyes were still glued to Trent's pale face. The medical team put him on a stretcher and ushered him to the ambulance; he was taken to the hospital.

Corinne sank to her knees, tears rolling down her cheeks. "Please don't leave me again, Trent." She sobbed.

"He is not going anywhere, Corinne," Sophia said gently. "Let's go to the hospital to bring him back."

It had been a long day, and Sophia's feet ache badly. By the time she had reached home, Naveen had already gone to sleep. She had asked him to go to bed as she had decided to take Janessa home and put her to bed after dinner. Naveen had asked if he was needed at the hospital, but both Corinne and Sophia thought he should stay back. Sophia had eaten a sandwich with Janessa, and then she just wanted to take a long shower.

As she stepped under the jet of warm water, her muscles began to relax. She realized that she had been trying to keep a strong front, but on the inside, she had been very scared, both for her best friend and her family. Now when she knew that everything was going to get better and that they all were safe and sound, she felt an urge to be held and comforted as well.

She poured some shampoo in her palm, but as she began rubbing her scalp, her hands were gently replaced by a stronger set of hands. She sighed deeply as Naveen's strong fingers made circles on her scalp, washing away the bubbles, along with all her stress. After thoroughly rinsing the shampoo away, Naveen planted a kiss on her shoulder and wrapped his arms around her belly. He was not wearing any clothes either; Sophia smiled at this.

"You smell delicious, like strawberries," he purred in her ear. "You know what I do to my strawberries? I eat them."

She felt his lips stretching near hers as he smiled, and without waiting for her response, he kneeled in front of her, placing his lips on the most delicate part of her. A moan escaped Sophia's mouth as she wound her fingers in Naveen's thick hair. He gently pushed her, so now she was leaning against the glass wall of the shower and pulled her fine legs apart to get better access to her. His tongue swirled around her sensitive spot, which made Sophia shiver delicately. Her hands reached for him to help keep herself steady as the coming orgasm washing over her made it difficult to maintain a standing position.

His mouth and tongue pushed Sophia to the edge of paradise, where she forgot all the worries and stress, and even her name. The only thing that mattered at the moment was Naveen and the pleasure he was bringing her. She did not even notice the moment when he stood up and pulled her into his arms. She only looked at him through hooded eyes as he carried her to the bedroom and gently landed her on the soft bed.

"I thought you might be exhausted...we can continue the rest of the action inside the bedroom," he murmured softly as his lips found hers. Sophia nodded with heavy eyelids, her hands snaking around his neck as she pulled him as close as she could. They were each other's solace, and Naveen had a plan to show it to Sophia in his own way.

Chapter Twelve

Trent opened his eyes slowly and squinted against the brightness of the room. He gradually adjusted to the lighting and turned his head to see his surroundings. He noticed a drip, a blood bag, a defibrillator and realized he was on a bed. Add two plus six, and he knew he was in a hospital.

His hand brushed against something hairy as he tried to sit up. He groaned as the pain shot from his chest to his back, and then he remembered. For a moment, he panicked, still struggling to get up. At that moment, Corinne stirred from her sleep and raised her head.

"Trent? You are awake!"

He looked at her but was not quite saw her. He kept trying to get up even though the pain was worsening with each movement.

"Hold on. Trent." She helped him up and adjusted his pillow. "Listen, calm down. You are alright. I'm here. You are safe, Trent. Look at me." She held his face in her hands. "You. Are. Safe." She emphasized each word looking straight into his eyes.

"Hamish," he whispered, his eyes wide like a kid.

"He's gone," she said, with a hint of happiness.

"What?" He looked confused.

"Yes, Trent. Frank, with the slick hair, is dead. The police came in just as he shot you." She explained in a hushed voice.

"But how am I still alive? He shot at me thrice. He-he shot at my head, didn't he?" Trent shook his head to clear the haze.

"No. He shot at you once. Only once—in your chest." Corinne pointed at his chest with her index finger. "The doctors said the bullet missed your heart and lodged itself in a muscle at your back. You were lucky in your bad luck. You are safe now, Trent. We are all safe. Hamish is no more." She hugged him awkwardly, trying not to cause him any more pain.

"Has he been confirmed as dead?" Trent asked again, as he had to be sure.

"Yes, Trent. He has," Corinne said softly. Her eyes probed his, and she could sense he had been scared beyond his wits. The fear was not related to his safety as much as it was to hers and their daughter's. She could understand the depth of his pain and the magnitude of his fear; she had about lost her mind as well. But now, she felt peace and knew it wouldn't be long before he felt it too.

"Where is Janessa?" he asked. His tense features were finally relaxing.

"She's with Sophia. They left about an hour ago. I told her to go since it was getting late, and Naveen might get worried."

"What time is it?"

"It's some few minutes past eight." There was a brief silence, and then she looked at his heavily bandaged chest. "Do you feel any pain?" she asked him.

"A little." He lied – it hurt like crazy.

"Should I get the doctor?"

"No, I'm fine. It's not so serious," he said, shifting a little, wincing sharply.

"I'll get the doctor." She insisted.

"No, Corinne. You don't need to." He sighed. "Just stay with me. That's all I need right now. Please."

She looked anxious for a moment but eventually sat down and held his hand in hers.

"I was really worried about you," he said.

"So was I. Janessa was the one who told me you had been in an accident." She shivered as she recalled the memory.

"Yes, my brakes failed at the last minute. It could only have been Hamish's doing. The accident was just his way of abducting me." Consciously, he was considering the fact that he had escaped death twice in one day. "How long have I been here?" he asked.

"Three days," she replied.

Three days, he thought. He could have been dead for three days already. The thought of it filled him with mixed emotions. He felt terrified about how close he had come to death – it had stared him in the face. He was dismayed at how abruptly life could be over; it could merely be a matter of seconds. But also, he was happy that he was alive and that Hamish was not. That alone gave him a reason to be thankful. He looked at Corinne for a long moment and smiled.

"What is it, Trent?" She frowned in confusion.

"I'm glad. Just glad." He sighed. "How did you find me?"

"The tracking device, all thanks to Janessa, who was the first to remember you had it. I would not have known where to start looking for you after combing all hospitals in the city."

"Hm. I owe her my life then."

"Why did Frank Hamish attack you? Is he someone you know? Have you both met before?" Corinne had so many questions, and she couldn't resist asking them now.

"No. We've never met, but I have met his close relatives and had gotten into trouble through an unsuspected mistake. He kept tabs on me for six years and stalked me to get revenge." He went on to narrate everything that had happened. Corinne was speechless, her lips slightly ajar in shock. He simply smiled and took her hand. "I'm glad it's all over now."

"What, what about the restaurant?" she asked hesitantly.

"I need to speak with Dubois." He sighed.

"You are not shutting it down, are you?"

"No. Just a small but important adjustment."

Jean Dubois was shocked beyond words. "*Mon ami*," he stated. "You had to endure all of this because of the restaurant."

"No, Dubois. Hamish simply had a very twisted mind. However, for now, let's take the Brussels sprouts soup off the menu."

"For how long, *mon ami?*"

"For as long as it doesn't get us in trouble. Maybe forever." Trent shrugged.

"I understand, Chef Martinez. This time around, we will be extra careful and even better."

Trent nodded in affirmation. This time, he would ensure there would be no more Hamishes. Not anymore, not today, and not ever.

After Dubois left, Trent felt hungry, and with the doctor's permission, Corinne fed him some broth with a spoon. Trent kept staring at her while she made some small talk to cheer him up.

"You know when I couldn't see you for three years, Corinne?" He grasped her wrist with the spoon and looked at her beautiful but tired face. "I wanted to come back as soon as I was well enough to walk, but I was scared."

"Scared? Of what?" Corinne was surprised he was bringing it up after all this time.

"That perhaps you might have started a new life with someone else. It was natural, you see. You had mourned us and were moving on, being the strong woman that you are." Corinne snorted at that.

"I loved you, Trent; I was only frustrated and mad at you for leaving me behind. But in all those years, I never thought about being with someone else. I focused all my energy on work." Trent pushed the hair back from her face and smiled.

"I am a lucky man, but I have already wasted three precious years of our life together. Promise me you will never leave me?" His voice went down to a whisper.

"I was not the one to leave, but okay." Corinne smiled and kissed his cheek. Nobody was coming to threaten their peace and happiness again.

Two weeks later.

Inspector Ryan got off the treadmill and snagged a bottle of water from a table nearby. It was day one of his week off, and he was determined to make the most of it. He took a long swig from the bottle, capped it, and put it back on the table. With a little towel draped across his neck, he headed for the bathroom.

"Hey, Ryan," a female voice called.

"Hey, Iris. What's up?" he asked as she was coming nearer. She was a regular visitor at the gym and was simply obsessed with keeping fit.

"Hot biceps." She winked while he crossed his arms.

"Thanks," he replied. It was a comment he got a lot. He sometimes wondered what went through people's minds whenever they gave him such comments. He was a police officer, and they could not possibly expect him to run after a thief if he wasn't fit.

"Are you free tonight? Maybe we could get a drink together. Whiskey on the rocks?" She suggested.

"Thanks, but I don't drink." He dropped quietly, waiting for her to leave.

"Oh," she said, her tone flanked with disappointment. "How about a movie then? We could go to a movie together."

"I'm sorry, but I've got…homework." He was lying, quite unsuccessfully.

She raised her eyebrows. Homework? Who still had homework at his age? He was what, thirty? Thirty-one?

Maybe more or a few years less, but certainly too old for homework. "Homework?" She laughed. "You've got to be kidding. You're an officer, Ryan, not a college student."

"Yeah, homework. I have got to clean the house, I've got to do some chores, I've got…stuff." He tried to explain, lying through his teeth. It was all he could do to keep his title as a gentleman, as he was beginning to feel sticky from sweating.

"Stuff," she said, obviously not believing him.

"Yeah, I've got a date." *Now, where had that come from?* he wondered. "There, I said it. I have a date with someone tonight." She furrowed her brows, scrutinizing his expression. He had said it so convincingly that she almost fell for it.

"A date. With whom?"

"Someone you don't know."

Iris rolled her eyes. "Is she hot?" she asked. He could see a spark of jealousy, and he decided to fan it hard.

"Absolutely. Drop-dead gorgeous. She used to be a model." He could see the coals catch fire. *Good job, Ryan. You are one heck of a terrible liar. Keep it going, and you'll be toast in no time.*

Iris's ears perked up at that. "Really? What product or company?"

Good. Now you have done it. Flip through the mental catalog. Curses Ryan, you're completely out of vogue! You know nothing about modeling.

Iris waved her hand in front of his eyes. "Hello! What product did she model for?"

"Um, lingerie. Swimsuits, bikinis, cosmetics." He listed. *Good job, Ryan; you have leveled up from novice to veteran. You just earned yourself a gold medal. Be sure to hang it in your office next week.*

He saw the look on her face and knew he didn't just have enough fire to grill steak; a whole forest reserve of jealousy was on fire. *Somebody call the fire department 'cause I'm out of here.*

"If you don't mind, Iris, I have to go and take a shower now. I'll catch up with you later," he said, just as he turned away on his heels. If she ever found out he had no date, much less a model, she'd be shooting lasers at him from her eyes until the end of the world.

"Any luck?" Eva asked.

"No. He says he has a date tonight," Iris replied as she was joining her friend at the cross-trainer.

"A date. Inspector Ryan has a date?" Eva said in disbelief. "Wow, I'll be a monkey's godmother."

"And she is a model," Iris added in jealous frustration.

"Really? For what product?"

"Everything that exposes. Lingerie, bikinis. I mean, he was all over her."

"I don't know about you, Iris. He may have pulled the wool over your eyes, but I don't think our man Ryan has a date." Eva tilted her head sideways thoughtfully. "How about we find out?"

"What? You want us to snoop on him? There is no way in this whole wide world that I'm doing that."

"Come on, Iris, don't be boring. It will be fun. We just want to find out if handsome Hercules has a date."

"And if he does?"

"Well, we'll set you up with someone else. If he doesn't, you still have a chance with him. As far as I know, Ryan Dakota has no girlfriend."

Ryan was lazily yawning as he stood up from his work table. He had been trying to connect some dots in a recent theft case, but all he got from it was a splitting headache and drowsy eyes. It was 5 p.m. He thought he deserved a nap before resuming his investigation. He heard a sudden noise from the trash can outside his house, but he didn't make anything of it. Had he gone to check it, he would have seen the two ladies, who could have easily passed off like thieves in their all-black outfit.

"Quiet down, Iris. He'll hear us!" Eva whispered.

"For the life of me, I still can't believe you talked me into doing this," Iris whispered back.

"Oh, just stop whining already; it's not like you can back out now."

"If we get caught, I am never listening to you again."

"Just shut up already. If we get caught, it will simply be because you won't stop talking."

"I can feel my bones shaking inside of me, Eva. It's cold. My joints will come out of their sockets."

Eva shook her head and sighed deeply. "That, my friend, is called fear. You are scared, not cold."

"My teeth are chattering."

"You are imagining things, Iris.

"I have a bad feeling about this. We should just leave."

"Come on, Iris. Don't be paranoid. What's the worst that could happen?"

"We'll get caught by someone in the neighborhood, mistaken for thieves because our outfits scream 'burglar,'" she said with air quotes, "and then we'll get sent off in front of a judge for an offense we did not even think about committing. That's the worst that could happen. We'll be lucky if he catches us himself. I'll just never show my face anywhere around him."

Eva held her head in exasperation. "Oh, Iris, you are such a windbag. Would you just hold that tongue for one minute and let me think?"

"Good. I could do that."

"Great. Now hand me the binoculars."

"I don't have them." Iris shrugged, her grey eyes dancing with fear.

"No, no, no. It's in the bag, Iris, in the bag."

"What bag?" Iris asked.

"What do you mean, what bag? I gave you a bag before we left the house."

"Oops," she said. She had dropped the bag on the table while looking for the keys and had forgotten to take it afterward.

"Is that an 'oops I forgot I have it,' or 'an oops I forgot it!'"

"Actually, I kind of forgot the bag back in the house; I left it on the table to look for the keys."

Eva sat in the dirt in resignation. "I give up. Remind me never to do this ever again."

"Definitely. Let's never do this again." Iris nodded.

"You forgot the bag!" she screamed silently. "How could you? Everything we needed was there. How could you have forgotten the bag? Without it, we practically don't have any business being here."

"You didn't tell me it was that important."

Eva hit her forehead with her palm in frustration. "How did I ever get stuck with you?" she groaned. Her response was met with a hiccup. "Are you having hiccups?"

Iris nodded. "I get them when I'm nervous, and seeing you angry makes me nervous."

"What?" She couldn't believe her ears. "I'm not angry with you; I'm just...urgh. It's no use explaining. Let's just get out of here." Eva looked around before standing up, only to see Iris standing already. She pulled her down in reflex. "What are you doing? Someone will see you."

"But you just said we should get out of here."

"Yes, I did, but not like that. Don't you know anything about sneaking out?" Iris shook her head. "Oh heavens, why have you saddled me with a friend like her? Just follow me," Eva said. She was beginning to leave when Iris tapped her. "What now?"

"I think we should leave in opposite directions."

"What? Why?" Eva asked, utterly befuddled.

"Well, you see, we are both dressed in black...."

"Again, with the color? It's winter, Iris; everyone wears dark colors. What does it matter whether we go left or right? Let us just get out of here," she said, pulling her along.

"I'm sorry," Iris said when they were back at the house.

"What about?"

"I really messed things up back there. I am not good at handling fear and nervousness. Sorry."

Eva sighed with a smile. "Lesson learned. I forgive you. Let's never do that again."

"I'll be sure to keep that in mind. Here is your bag." She picked it from the table and held it out to her.

"Thanks. I'll be leaving now. See you tomorrow."

"Bye," Iris replied, sitting down heavily on the sofa as Eva shut the door behind her.

Drizella picked up her phone for the fifth time to put a call through to Ryan. Each time she had decided against it, merely ending up dropping the phone. She redialed his number and jumped a little as it began to ring. She was not sure she wanted to tell him, but she felt it would be fair if he knew about it.

"Hello." His voice was slurred and evidently sleepy. She contemplated hanging up when he spoke again. "Driz, are you there?"

"Hey," she said softly. "Are you busy?"

"No. just taking an afternoon nap. Are you alright?"

"Can we talk?" she asked, finding his sleepy voice amusing.

"Right now?" he asked, sounding more alert.

"Well, if you are free, we can meet somewhere." There was a brief pause and a stifled yawn.

"Sure, no problem. We can talk over dinner then," he said.

"Good. See you when?"

"In an hour? I'll come to pick you up."

"Alright." She hung up and held the phone a moment before standing up. She did not know why, but for the first time in a long time, she felt like dressing up. She threw her wardrobe doors opened and did a quick scan. Her azure blue dress was the way to go, so she picked it up and dug out her jewelry box. It would make her day if the last image he had of her were in something more beautiful and feminine than the prison wears. She waited for him while she styled her hair and dug out a popping red lipstick. She felt like a runway model; she once used to be; only this time, she had an audience of one-Ryan.

Her sunflower-shaped diamond earrings glittered in the light as she stepped out of the house. Ryan almost whistled; her beauty was one he had not seen in a long time. Her black hair and light brown skin only made it all the more apparent. He could almost say she was doing a catwalk for him, with her steps slow and measured as if telling him to note every detail. He was right, after all; he had a date with a drop-dead gorgeous model. He could already pick the scent of her perfume before she reached him. It was nothing but arousing. He couldn't help but wonder what she was up to.

"Hi," she said when reaching him.

"Hi. You look beautiful." He complimented.

"You don't look half bad yourself," she said, with a smile that set off a rock and roll band in his head. *Amazing,* he thought to himself. Here he was at thirty-one with butterflies in his tummy, and that too for a woman who carried an aura of mystery. *Way to go, Ryan, she has you nailed. There's no escaping this one.* He opened the door for her and went around to the other side of the car. He wondered what she wanted to say and why it would be a good enough cause for her to really glam up. He had never thought he would see her that way, and she seemed to do it deliberately, as there was a little smile playing at the corner of her lips throughout the drive. Her eyes looked distant, though, and he hoped there was no bad news.

Chapter Thirteen

The diner place was not too crowded. It had a friendly atmosphere and slow music in the background; it was just perfect. She had picked that restaurant deliberately as it was her favorite place to relax and to think. They had ordered food, but she had little appetite. She simply twirled her fork around in her plate, oblivious of Ryan's concerned stare.

"Why are you not eating?" he asked eventually.

She shrugged and sighed deeply. "I'm not hungry."

"The food is really nice." He scooped a forkful from his plate and held it out to her. "Try it. Go on." He urged. He watched her mouth close on the fork and waited for her response.

"Mmh. You're right." She nodded.

"So, dig in." He gestured with his fork as he continued eating. They both cleared the plate in no time and then waited, with patient silence, expecting someone to break the ice.

"So," Ryan began, clearing his throat. "You said you wanted to see me, and you wanted to talk."

"Yes." She nodded, looking everywhere but at him.

"Alright. What about? I'm all ears." He adjusted his seat and placed his glass of water carefully aside.

"Me," she said. "It's about me."

"Are you doing alright?" he asked, suddenly apprehensive.

"I am. I am perfectly fine. I just…it's…well, I…."

"You can tell me, Drizella. You can tell me anything." He put his hand on hers and squeezed it gently.

"It's just. I didn't want you finding out later or elsewhere; I mean, I owe you that much, considering the efforts you put into getting me out of jail. I owe you a lifetime, Ryan, a lifetime." She paused to see if he was following. "It would be selfish of me if I didn't tell you that

I'm leaving the country. Permanently," she said. There was a long pause.

"I'm sorry, what?" He stared at her blankly for a long moment.

"I'm leaving the country, Ryan. I'm going home to Tanzania." She emphasized each word carefully.

"What? I mean, what like, since when have you taken that decision?" He furrowed his brows, not quite understanding his own emotions.

"A couple of days ago."

"Whoa." He felt as though someone had knocked the air out of him. He did not expect that, not in a million years. "Thanks…for, err, telling me. I mean, I feel…I feel honored. It's a pleasure to be told such great news. That's fantastic. When are you leaving then?" His voice was shaky; it was like he thought something else, but those words lost their way to his mouth, and instead, some others blurted out.

"Next week." The reply hit him worse than the news.

"What? Next week? You mean this coming Monday, next week?" He wished that he had heard her wrong.

"Yes," she said softly.

"Awesome." The dinner idea suddenly felt weird. "Can we go outside for a moment? It is getting too hot in here." He stood up and followed her as they walked outside. There was a wooden balcony that led to the back of the diner. The balcony overlooked a lake and the outer section of the diner for those who preferred the night outdoors. The balcony was rather vast and had the reflection of lights from the outer side of the diner. Her silver stiletto clicked away on the wooden floor as they walked to the end of the balcony. Ryan rested on the railings and sighed, saying nothing. At least he was able to connect these dots. The dress-up, the catwalk, the dinner, it was all her way of saying goodbye. The goodbye he did not want. The goodbye he wasn't ready to accept. The goodbye he was never going to be able to say because he knew now that he did not want to hear a goodbye from her at all. He did not wish to just be friends. He did not want to be the policeman she was indebted to; he wanted more. He wanted her to be his.

Drizella did not know what to say. She had not expected him to react that way. She thought he would take it well, but instead, he had been shocked to hear it. Music wafted from inside the diner, making the tense situation even worse. It was slow and sounded like a farewell song. Ryan lifted off the wooden railings, taking her hand and pulling her away from it.

"Dance with me, Drizella," he said and then swayed rhythmically with the song. Her body was a perfect fit for his as they let the song take them on a ride. "Let us enjoy this moment because I want to remember everything when you leave. I want to remember today and how beautiful you looked in this dress and how every step you took toward me had my name in it. I want to remember this evening and remember that I danced with you, right here, and that every second was magical." His voice was merely a whisper. They both were so close that they could hear and count each other's heartbeats.

"I'm sorry, Ryan."

"Shh, no apologies." He put his index finger on her plump lips. "Just enjoy the moment. We may never get another." The music had stopped, but they kept on dancing until they finally came to an end.

Drizella closed her eyes and sighed. Did he know how hard he was making things for her by acting this way? Expressing his outright displeasure was better than his silence. "Ryan, please say something."

"Like what?" he asked, holding her in an embrace. This was where he wanted her to be; in his arms. Not in Tanzania or anywhere else, but with him.

"I know you're not happy," she said, finally.

"Absolutely." He shrugged as if he was stating an obvious fact.

"But you are not saying so." She sounded frustrated.

"Deliberately."

"Why not?" She wanted to step back to look at his face, but he held her still. She tried again, but he wouldn't let her. She wriggled free eventually, but his look only puzzled her. "What is on your mind, Ryan?"

"You," he said after a brief silence. "You are on my mind because I want to etch your name on my heart forever." His words only pricked her. She had to leave the country; she had no reason to stay back. Except maybe him, but she wasn't sure she was ready to admit that.

"Stop doing this to me, Ryan," she whispered, still in controlled frustration. He held the side of her face and smiled. It was a smile that was louder than any decibel of noise. She understood. It was a conflict between his head and his heart. If he chose his head, it would be easier for her to leave, but if he chose his heart, she might live with the guilt for the rest of her life.

It might have been sudden and unexpected, but she wanted it as much as he did. He kissed her with all he had. His feelings all poured into one single action that couldn't capture it all. She allowed him because the hunger was mutual, and the desire was equal. The two of them had to fight, both their heads and their hearts. He somehow knew what her answer would be, that he might not be successful.

"Stay with me, Drizella. Stay with me. Don't leave. I want you to be mine forever. Stay," he pleaded.

"I'm sorry," came as a reply. He said nothing afterward. Even after he dropped her at her house, he said good night, but not goodbye because he knew he would never be able to tell her goodbye, not today. Not ever.

The week went by slowly and very swiftly at the same time. He had tried not to think about her and trained harder at the gym, staying longer than he used to. He pored over the case he had, but he still could not crack it. Every day he wounded up with a headache from stretching himself too much. He looked at the date as it got nearer, filling him with a dread he could not explain. The new week began, and he resumed work. He masked it well and poured his attention into his work. He woke up on Wednesday morning, with a part of him hoping she would not leave. He counted the hours as they ticked away. It was supposed to be an afternoon flight, and by the evening, as he returned from work, he decided goodbye wasn't a myth afterward; it was as real as the sky above him.

As he got out of his car and turned toward the house, a taxi repeatedly honked to get his attention. He looked up and wondered what the noise was all about. The occupant of the car got down and once again walked toward him. A catwalk that had his name all over it and a smile that sent butterflies fluttering in his stomach.

"Drizella," he said in disbelief.

"I'm walking for you, Ryan; this is not goodbye. Can I stay?" she asked as she reached him.

"I thought you would never ask," he said in glee as he picked her up and wheeled around excitedly. "You are welcome to stay."

"Forever?"

"Forever," he replied and once again kissed her, a warm welcome in its purest form. It filled a void that had long existed inside of them. Needless to say, Cupid aimed his shots well. Bull's eye.

Rick pressed the doorbell and waited. He had been on a business trip for three weeks and was just getting back home. In his absence, a lot had happened, which he had been told. Naveen had given him updates on just about everything that had happened. He remembered Hamish and knew what he was capable of – just what he had done. He could have said people never do really change, but then there was the news about Drizella. Perhaps people do change. Hamish was only an exception, and now he was six feet under. *Good riddance*, he thought.

The door clicked and then opened. He greeted the face that popped out with a broad smile.

"Hi," he said as he stepped into the house. "Did you miss me?" he asked, kissing Bella softly.

"Mmh. It was lonely without you. There was not so much to do. No one to talk to. It's just me and the walls…and furniture—no one else. Maybe the dog, but it doesn't talk much," she said, with a slight shrug. His eyes were tender; he understood the words she left unsaid.

"You have been thinking about it again, Bella," he said concernedly.

"No, it's not that. I just missed you, that's all."

"Really, Bella?"

"How was your trip?" she asked, trying to avoid the discussion she had unintentionally started. She did not want him feeling bad.

"Bella."

"I didn't have to mention that; I mean, we talked on Skype virtually every day. I should not have said that. I'm sorry." She looked down.

He dropped his suitcase on the floor beside him and straightened himself to hold her arms. "Bella, my love. I'm here now. You don't have to feel so lonely anymore. And my business trip was fine, and I'm back with you. Alright?"

She nodded silently and smiled. "I'm glad you are now back. Come on, go on and take a shower; I'll fix dinner," she said and left hurriedly.

Rick watched her go with a sigh and scratched the back of his head at a loss of what to do. This wasn't exactly the kind of welcome he was anticipating. He had been gone for three weeks; not the longest time he had been away since the six years that they had been married. However, it was long enough though to stoke fires and reawaken thoughts and wishes. "Not again," he said silently.

Naveen held his chin, his mind in deep thought and his elbow on the arm of his chair. This was the worst winter he had ever experienced. He was beginning to get worried, as the way problems were cropping up one after the other. Maybe a magician with a glowing ball had them all in a cauldron. First, it was him with Sophia, where his ex-wife was all out to get them. Then it was Trent who barely escaped taking a dunk in the waters of death. And now, it was Rick looking anything but cheerful. He cleared his throat and sat up to look at Rick straight in the eye.

"So, let me get this straight. You go on a business trip for about three weeks, returned yesterday, and have your wife go ballistic on you," he ratted.

"No, not ballistic," Rick said calmly. "She has started overthinking things, Naveen, and it is making me worried. I mean, I knew she did not plan to say that, but it was there, in her voice."

"She is bound to overthink things," Naveen stated.

"I was away for three weeks, Naveen. Just three. Those were weeks, not months."

"That is pretty much enough time to think if you ask me. It took Sophia three weeks to think about running away when she found out she was pregnant," he said, watching Rick shake his head tiredly. "Your wedding anniversary is in four days, Rick. You will have been married six years in four days. You know how women overthink."

"But I'm not bothered…." Rick started saying.

"Hold on, what's your name?"

"What?"

"What is your name?"

"Rick," he replied, obviously confused.

"Great, and what is her name?"

"Um, Bella?"

"Exactly. She's Rick, and you are Bella…oh, I mean, you are Rick, and she is Bella; you are two different people. You are not bothered, but she expressly is. And she might go ballistic anytime soon." Naveen noted.

Rick was silent for a moment. "I know she is bothered, and one could say she has every right to be. While she may be hiding a lot of pain, she is not talking to me about it. I mean, she probably might have, and I probably did not pay attention." Rick mused.

"Does not look like things will go that way for long. Six years without kids, let me tell you, man, that is a lot for a woman. You can feel cool about it and try talking her out of thinking. But she has eyes, Rick. She has friends that have children. She sees kids at the park. They are all over the mall. She sees pictures…she's counting the days, Rick."

"We could consider adoption," Rick said, with a frustrated shrug.

"Last time you told me you mentioned that to her, she blew up the roof."

"But I don't know what the problem is! Santa does not give children to childless couples, does he? Maybe we could write to him a 'Dear Santa' since Christmas is next month."

"What did the doctor say?" Naveen asked coolly.

"Nothing. The doctor said we are both fine, so there is nothing wrong. The kids will come when they feel like it." He put his hands up in the air in confused defeat.

Naveen paused for a while to study his friend. He had been with him long enough to know there was something he was not saying.

"Riccardo Anderson," he started saying. "We have been together for about thirty-three years now, and so you can put on a façade in front of everybody but not me. I know you, Rick, and I know very well when you are hiding something. What is the matter? You are not really not bothered, aren't you?" he added, knowing that he had just hit the nail on the head.

Rick sighed heavily. "I don't know, Naveen. I try not to think about it. I am worried, and that's the truth. But worrying solves nothing as far as I know. So, I try not to think about it, and while it's working for me…to a fair extent, I'm not so sure I can say the same about Bella."

Sophia opened the door to the study and stepped in silently. "Sorry to interrupt your conversation, but the postman brought a package and said he wouldn't let anyone sign it but you."

"What's in the package?" Naveen asked, seemingly curious.

"I don't know. He did not tell. But he is insisting on seeing you. And Rick."

"Why does he want to see me? How would he know I was here?"

Sophia shrugged in obvious ignorance. "He is not talking." The men rose after hearing that.

"Where is he?"

"He is downstairs."

"Alright. Let's go," Naveen said as they stepped out of the study.

Drew was waiting outside the house patiently. He was not in a hurry. *Time changes so many things*, he mused. A lot had happened in ten years; a lot had changed in less. He had heard many stories; he had seen it on the news and followed up as much as he could. At last, he found his runaway brother, or if he were to be more honest, he was the one who had run away. He doubted if either of them would recognize him or him, them. Ten years. He wondered why he came back. Perhaps he was tired of running, or he just wanted to pay a visit, he couldn't say. His outfit had worked; the face cap especially did well to hide his face. The woman who opened the door to see him must have been Naveen's wife, he guessed.

"You said you wanted to see me," someone said behind him as he had been standing with his back to the door. He turned around to see Naveen standing with arms folded. He wore a grey sweatshirt and had rolled up his sleeves, making his stance menacing. His face cap still shielded his face, so they could not see him. Raising his head a little, he could see that Rick had the same stance. They had grown so fast; he could barely recognize them.

"Yes," he replied. "I have a package for both of you."

Rick looked around and craned his neck to look behind Drew. "I don't see any package."

"Yes, because the package... is me," Drew replied, taking off the face cap.

Rick gaped in shock. The sandy brown hair, the same square face, the same coffee brown eyes. It could only be one person. "Drew?" Rick took a step forward. "Drew. It's you?" he stuttered in surprise, looking at Naveen, whose face was equally plastered with shock. "Naveen...it's...it's Drew. It's my brother, Drew!"

"Drew," Naveen repeated. "Andrew Anderson," he said again. "Best baseball player of the year, Lincolnshire high school. Second best graduating student, twelve years ago, Department of Economics, University of Chicago. The school that has fielded 12 Nobel prize laureates in economics—more than any other university! What a surprise. So many questions are now coming to mind…it has been how many years now, ten? Still, good to see you," Naveen said, moving to envelop him in a bear embrace, with tons of question marks in his eyes.

"It feels equally good to see you two," Drew said as he disengaged from the hug. "And I take this dashing beauty here is your wife?"

"Absolutely." Naveen grinned. "Her name is Sophia." He motioned for her to come close and enclosed her in a side hug.

Drew smiled and extended his hand for a handshake. "Nice to meet you. I'm Drew."

"It is a pleasure meeting you. I never knew Rick had a brother."

"Oh, he does quite alright. I have just not been around much. I just decided to pay a visit. Feels good to be back in the states. How is that little bun in the oven doing?" Drew said, smiling.

"Perfectly fine." Sophia returned. Rick looked confused.

"He means the baby," Sophia explained, clarifying his confusion. He made a silent 'oh' and nodded his head.

"Where have you been all these years, Drew?" Rick asked when they were back in the study.

"It's a long story. I have been all over the place, moving from state to country, from the countryside, and back to the city. I have been living like a nomad. Here today, there the next day. But I got tired of running around and decided to come back home and find myself a bearing."

"You still dance and spray paint, do you?"

"Paint, yes. Dance, not anymore. Man, I am getting old. The world is a place full of opportunities, and dancing is not something I look forward to doing anymore. Back then, when I was young and foolish, I could flout the rules and defy dad's orders and still get away with it. But getting tangled with Frost and Marshawn changed things. They were then out for my head. I just had to run and let the dust settle. I mean, I do graffiti because I love to paint, not because I want to ruin white washings or give the president's posters a funky looking mustache and hair."

"So, you still do graffiti?" Rick mused. Naveen had left the two of them together, so they could talk and catch up on the years. He disappeared, reasoning that he had several calls to receive; however, in fact, he had gone out to join Sophia on the terrace.

Drew shrugged. "Anytime I feel like it. I just paint now. I'm a full-time artist. All that talent just could not go to waste; I had to find a way to make good use of it."

"Dad never wanted you to paint. He had always thought you were wasting time painting."

"Dad never did understand either of his children. I graduated second best, not because I wanted to. You know me, calculations and theories are not my things. But I needed to prove to dad that I could be an artist and still have a good degree."

"You did not stay long enough to understand how proud he was of you."

"Staying meant trouble. Frost wanted to frame me for his crime; I could not wait that out. But I'm glad I fled, as I learned, and I grew. I met people. I made mistakes, did stupid things. I got into trouble, blamed me, and got back on my feet." He paused for a while. "My painting earned me fame and good money, but you know what, I never really felt satisfied."

"So, you decided to come back home. Permanently?"

"Maybe." He shrugged with uncertainty.

"When did you arrive?"

"Yesterday. Lodged in a guest house downtown. Might visit dad sometime during the week. Want to come with me?"

"Absolutely."

"I am also looking forward to meeting your wife. You are married, aren't you?"

"I am. Found yourself one yet?" Rick asked with an impish grin.

"Not yet. I'm a lone wolf, man. Lone wolf," he repeated for emphasis.

"Could not find one in ten years?" Rick said with a surprised chuckle.

"I almost did, but we broke up. Good riddance. She wanted all my money, swallowed a sword up to its hilt. I walked. That was a long time ago."

"Cool, maybe we can find you one now that you're around."

"I am not so sure this was a plan I had on my min..." Drew shook his head. "Enough about me, let us talk about you. How has it been with you? How many kids yet? I am guessing two."

"I've been great. Work is awesome. I have been getting more contracts, some that I have deferred because they are getting way too much for me, and I need a break from traveling around all the time. And the kids...well, they will come soon. Taking their time wherever it is babies come from."

"Hold on, how many years have you been married?" a frown creased his forehead.

"Six years in four days," Rick drawled, wondering why the topic had to come up again.

"Whoa. That is a lot. How's your wife taking it?"

"Bad." There was a long pause. "Can we talk about something else? It's getting unnerving thinking about it."

Drew looked at his brother with deep scrutiny; he could already see that things weren't good. He decided to let go of the subject and then switched topics. "Tell me about your job," he said eventually, mentally digging through his head in search of his investigative mode. Perhaps, he would be staying longer than he intended, he mused.

Chapter Fourteen

One month later.

Bella looked up at the hospital sign before stepping out of her car. The strain between her and Rick had only grown from bad to worse, and although she could see that he was trying to make her happy and had deferred a contract to a friend so he could stay with her, it did not help. No matter how hard she tried, she felt herself withdrawing from him. She gladly wallowed in the waters of self-pity and shut Rick out. She justified her actions to herself - she needed time to think and to clear out her head. She still loved Rick; she did not doubt it. She loved him with all of her being, and she knew he would fight a bear with bare hands just for her.

However, she simply could not find a way to get out of her self-imposed mental torture. She had taken a test a few days back and was now afraid to hear what the report would say.

She had barely walked up the stairs to the doctor's office when she heard her name. She looked up and saw Sophia.

"Hi Sophia," she said, flashing a bright smile.

"Hello, Bella, it's so good to see you. How have you been?"

"Alive. I've been alive. You're here for a check-up?"

"Yes. What about you?"

"To see the doctor," Bella grinned.

"Are you not feeling too well?" Sophia frowned.

"I'm perfectly fine. I just need to get a test report. I'll hurry on now."

"Alright. I'll see you around," Sophia said, skipping down the stairs. Had Sophia been there about thirty minutes later, she would have seen Bella's smile gone sour and her eyes turn red. She would have heard a chuckle stifled by sobs and laughter of unbelief and one word: cancer.

Rick knew something had snapped, but he did not know what. There was a strain; he understood that. But who put scissors in the strain? He could not figure it out. He was losing his mind, that was for certain. He felt cut off, ignored, neglected. He was losing his wife, and that was something he could not handle. She had just come back from somewhere and would not say wherever it was, and he could almost hear a twine snap. His questions of two days ago were met with silence and pallor. He could not concentrate on his work.

He stood up from his office table and loosened his tie. Cursing under his breath, he scratched his head in frustration and growled. She could have helped him out by telling him what exactly was going on. That would be saving him a lot of stress and mental stretching.

He pulled out his chair and sat in it again. His head began a rhythmical throbbing that worsened as he continued to stare at the laptop screen, unable to concentrate. He closed the laptop with a heavy clamp and slowly rested his head on his arms, lying down on his large table.

He thought of ringing the doorbell and wait for her to come to him, hoping she would finally say something. The door clicked, but she did not pull it open for him. He sighed and pushed the door open by himself. She was already headed for the bedroom. He lengthened his strides, covering the distance, and catching her by the arm.

"Let go of me, Rick." She struggled with him. Her voice was hoarse, as though she had been screaming at the top of her lungs.

"Not until you tell me what is going on, right here and right now. What is going on with you? Did something happen that I don't know about? Did someone say something to you? Did you lose a friend? A relative? Talk to me, Bella. Don't shut me out like this," he asked her softly.

"I don't want to talk to you," she shot.

Rick winced, his hand falling to his side. Hot tears burned at the back of his eyes, but he could not cry. The words stung, but he doubted if she realized it. He tried to say something, but words would not form; they were just a salty lump in his throat instead. He tried again. Nothing.

Bella looked away, stifling the pain. She knew she was hurting him, but she couldn't bring herself to tell him what was wrong. She wanted to tell him a lot of things, but she could not muster the courage to do so. "I'm sorry, Rick. I just can't tell you anything despite how badly I want to."

"Bella," he started again. "Whenever you feel you are ready to talk, I will be right here, waiting." His smile pierced her like a long saber.

"I do not mean to hurt you, Rick," she sobbed inwardly. "Excuse me," she said, leaving him standing there in the corridor, forlorn and heartbroken. She was consumed by self-pity and utterly confused. She thought maybe she would even lose her mind, just as she was possibly going to lose her life. She locked the door behind her and sobbed hysterically. Her head swam with different thoughts, several crazy ones. Fear took wings from pessimism. It grew and filled her with dread, to the point where she forgot about everything for a moment. Maybe even longer. She forgot she had two options - facing her health problem head-on and telling Rick about it, then trying to enjoy the last few months she had. That was on the brighter side. Or, she would find herself sinking into a depression. Death would come either way - if she did not treat her cancer soon. Perhaps sooner one way, or a little later the other way.

So loud were her fears and the shadows that danced a luau in front of her eyes that she couldn't hear Rick knocking on the door. Or when he switched from knocking on it to hitting it with increasing force. It was nothing but a nightmare she so badly wanted to wake up from, except she was not sleeping. Was she even thinking? She wondered. She could tell Rick that blood cancer had a cure. Chemotherapy was an option. She could get treated. But she was scared of him. She was scared he would not be able to handle it. She could not tell him. She wouldn't. She had to keep it away from him, even if he was going to hate her for it.

"Open the door, Bella!" Rick yelled, hitting it with clenched fists. "Bella, can you hear me? Please open this door, or I break it down. Are you listening to me, Bella?" There was no sound, no movement. "Bella!"

Was she even in the room at all? He moved back a distance, preparing to come at with full force. He hit the door and fell through into the room, hitting the ground with a terrible thud, as she had opened it at the exact same time. He looked up at her before he got up. Frowning, he held his left shoulder.

"Have you been crying?"

She shook her head and turned away from him. "You can have the room; I'll stay in the guest room."

"What?" Was she even listening to herself? Did she know the extent of the damage she was causing to their relationship acting this way? Did she not know she was hurting him? Did she not know she was pushing him away? Oh wait, she knew. She was doing it deliberately; else, she would not be acting this way. "Bella. Why? Why are you doing this?"

"I am not doing anything."

"You are doing many things! A lot of things!"

"I am not having this conversation with you."

"You are," he grounded, blocking her exit. "Spill. I'm listening."

"I'm tired, alright? And I want to rest, move aside, Rick."

"Wow, Bella. This is great, just great. Not a problem. Look." He moved to the bed and grabbed his pillow and a duvet.

Please stay, Rick. Don't leave. Ask me one more time, just ask one more time.

"You can have the room," he came up with, putting up his free hand. "I'm leaving. I'll let you have your moment. When you feel like talking to me, I'll be in the next room," he simply said. His jaw tightened, and he forced a smile. *Please tell me to stay. Don't just watch me leave.*

Stay Rick. Please stay, she thought to herself. If only they could hear each other's thoughts.

"Good night, Bella," he said and left, feeling more miserable than ever.

I tried Rick, I tried. But I don't have the courage. Please, forgive me.

Naveen worked late into the night at the office. His desk was filled with reports and orders and suggestions and what-not. His mail was spilling over with piled-up e-mails. He had to work double-time to cover much ground. As his wall clock chimed at 9 o'clock, he raised his head from the desk and knew that his phone would start ringing in no time. If it weren't from Frances, it would be from Sophia. He picked his phone and switched it to silent mode. He did not want to be disturbed. If he could get seventy percent of his work done, that would be a huge reduction of his burdensome workload.

His neck hurt from the posture of sitting he had maintained for hours. He took a break and stood up to stretch and walk around. He did a few minutes of muscle-relaxing exercises and then paused. His phone lighted up, drawing his attention. He had a text message from Sophia. *"Come home now; Rick is here."* Frowning in confusion, he made an exaggerated sigh, slightly annoyed that he was being interrupted from his work. He weighed his options; could he leave his work for Rick? And why was Rick at his house at this time of the night? He should probably call home. Seeing Rick could not be that urgent, could it? On second thought, he arranged his desk neatly, shut down his laptop, and picked up his keys. He would have to resume extra early tomorrow. He put his laptop into his briefcase and left the office.

Rick stood up as Naveen walked into the house. He staggered a little before regaining his composure. "Naveen!" he said loudly, "good to see you. I have been waiting just for you."

Naveen paused in motion, uncertainty clouding his eyes. Something was not right. "Rick? Are you drunk?"

"He is. Very drunk," Sophia declared.

"Rick? Why?" Rick was not a fan of alcohol. He had never been. Why did he get so drunk? "What happened?" Naveen asked again.

"Bella has left me." He rasped as he walked toward the door, stepping out into the chilly air. His head was full of so many raging thoughts, while he was blaming himself for her having to leave. Had he had known, he would have stayed with her yesterday instead of leaving the room. He would have probed her further, asked her what was going on. He would have told her he cared. He would certainly not have left the room. He would have stayed and made sure she would finally talk, and they would have settled whatever was wrong. He should have stayed. But he did not, and so she packed her things and left before he arrived from work a few hours ago. He thought he was going to go crazy. He could no longer think. He could barely breathe. He could not understand anything. He had railed and turned the room upside down before driving around the city without thinking about where he was going. How he avoided getting caught for drunk driving, he did not want to know. He had somehow found his way to Naveen's house and sat outside the door until Sophia convinced him to come into the house.

"She has left me," he whispered, standing in the cold. "She is not coming back. She said she is not coming back."

"Do you really believe that?" Naveen asked, standing behind him.

"I do not know what to believe anymore. Or what not to believe. Something I know nothing about? I don't understand anything. She didn't tell me anything. She kept pushing me away, and she never told me anything."

"What happened?" Naveen asked concernedly.

"I don't know. She packed and left without warning. No signal. I could feel us stray away from each other recently. I felt the strain; I heard it snap. I should have stayed. I should have stayed with her."

"You cannot beat yourself up if you do not exactly know why she is acting that way."

"I wish I did."

"You can't take a guess?" It sounded more like a statement of fact than a question.

"No. It's not about kids; I know it's not. It's more than that. There is something else. But I don't know what." He seemed to be getting soberer.

"Have you tried her line?"

"It's switched off. She put it off. She…" he was too pained to find words and make full sentences. He crumpled to the floor on his knees and keeled over. He was silent for a long time; his fist clenched on the cold floor.

Seeing Rick like this scared Naveen. Rick was not one to lose control of himself, but though he could handle losses or accept failure, or even handle losing contracts to someone of a much lower level than his, losing his wife was something he could not handle. It would break him. Naveen felt his pain, wishing he could help him. He opened his mouth to say something but decided against it. He figured that asking him if he knew where she might be would only amount to nothing. He was still slightly drunk and probably, or most definitely, not thinking straight.

Rick stood up and started walking. Naveen caught his shirt and drew him back. "Where are you going?"

"Home," he simply replied.

"I am not letting you go home by yourself in this state."

"What's the worst that could happen? I will get caught for drunk driving, pay a small fee..."

"And earn yourself a bad reputation. You are a well-known architect, Rick; a bad name will not look good on you. Hold on; I'll drive you. Let me get my keys."

"I'll drive myself," Rick insisted stubbornly.

"No. you can't, and you won't. Stay right here and don't move," he said firmly. He took a few steps toward the house and then looked back. "Don't move."

"Aye, aye, captain," Rick replied, sounding drowsy.

A few days later

Drew made lazy strokes on the canvas with his paintbrush and looked at his work; it looked odd. It seemed like he had overpainted a particular color. He moved a few steps back so that he could get a clearer picture of the painting. He picked up his brush and touched the dollop of red acrylic paint he had squeezed out on a piece of plastic paper, holding on for a moment before he applied it to the painting, blending it with the rest. He dipped the brush in a little bowl of water that was already turning several shades of different hues and dragged it across the canvas.

"Almost there. Just a little bit more. A stroke of orange, some bit of feathery cobalt blue, a tint of sunset yellow, make that a smidge of dove brown, a slight shade of black. Perfect," he said to himself, taking the paintbrush away from the canvas in a dramatic manner.

"Hi Dad," he whispered to himself, grinning at the portrait he had just finished. Someone else would have thought he had painted himself. He was that much of his father's spitting image. "It has been a while. I'll see you in a few days. Just a few more days," he said with a contented sigh, bending backward to stretch his back. His white apron was a splash of different colors, as it wasn't the first time he was using it. A similar one hung on a wall just beside the door. It held his memories, every country he had been to, countries he had painted in. The breeze was blowing in through the window, scattering some papers off the table and onto the floor. His room overlooked the main road, and his floor gave him a great view of the city below. There was a restaurant just across the street, and a stationery store, amidst other local businesses. He had somehow managed to get an apartment with the help of an old friend, and he knew he should always be thankful. It was simply manna (God-sent); he did not work for it, and yet he got so much out of it.

He picked up the sheets of paper that had landed on the wooden floor and placed them back on the table with a heavy object on them. "You stay right here," he said to the stack of papers as though it could lift the object he had placed on it. He went ahead to close the window, pausing to look out a little bit, and suddenly squinted to make sure he was seeing right. He grabbed a pair of binoculars from the table next to him and took another look. He had seen right. "Bella," he whispered in surprised relief. He had found her, without even having to look for her; she was there, going into the restaurant across from his place. He removed his apron and hurried to wash his hands and change his clothes, hoping she would still be there when he arrives. He sped down the three flights of stairs from his floor and waited at the last one to let a neighbor pass. He nodded a good morning and scooted through the door.

"Morning, Mr. Drew," the newspaper guy called out.

"Morning, little Smith. How's it going?" he returned to the kid without waiting to get a reply. Crossing the street as soon as the traffic allowed for it, he headed straight for the restaurant. He reached into his pocket for his phone but could not find it. He felt his pockets and patted for it in a frenzy. No luck, he had forgotten to take it. He spotted her car and sighed in relief; she had not left yet.

"Alright, Drew, compose yourself. You don't have to go in there looking like a hitman is after you."

He breathed in deeply and walked more calmly, making it seem like a casual stroll as if he had indeed intended to come to that restaurant. He scouted through the glass, trying to see her before going in. She was seated alone at a table, at a corner of the dining room where no one could bother her. *Good. Works in my favor.* He mused and went through the door, then picked up a menu list from an empty table and walked over to hers.

"Do you mind if I join you?" he asked.

She did not pay much attention to the voice or who was talking to her, or else she would have looked up right away. She shrugged casually. "Not a problem," she said, without looking up from the menu she had in her hands.

"Great. Thanks." He sat down with a slight smile. A dimple played at the corner of his cheek. The menu list was big enough, so he hid his face behind it. "What are you ordering?"

Bella looked up then but couldn't see his face. Was that any of his business? "I'm yet to decide," she answered.

"Everything looks so tempting. I heard the food is nice here. Is this your first time?" Drew asked without taking away his menu list.

Bella blinked, trying to hold her tongue. Was she really going to sit here with this chatterbox? If he asked another question, she would leave the table. She wanted to avoid people like him, which was why she picked that table. But apparently, one of them found his way there. She dropped her menu on the table with a slightly loud splat. "No, it is not my first time here."

"Wow. Well, then you should have a favorite dish, am I right? Maybe you can help me make a choice as well. I seem to be at a loss of what to pick."

Bella twisted her mouth in controlled frustration. Would anyone know where human-pest repellents are sold? This fellow here needs to be sprayed. And why was he hiding his face behind the menu list? Was he hiding from someone? Could he be stalking her? She looked around for another empty table and picked her bag, ready to get up.

Drew heard the keys jingle. *"Attention fully secured. Switch to the next level."* He waited for her to stand up and be about to leave before he put down his menu.

"Bella," he called gently.

The voice had a familiar resonance. There was only one person she knew that called her name that way, maybe a little deeper than that, and that was Rick. Could he? She wheeled around sharply, her brown tresses covering her face for a few seconds before she pushed them back into place. It was not Rick; it was his look-alike elder brother, Drew.

"Drew?" He had her attention, one hundred percent unless she decided to walk out on him, which he hoped she would not do.

"Nice to see you, too," he grinned, just like Rick.

Nice to see her? She was not pleased to see him! Rick had probably sent him. And how on earth did he find her? "Listen. If Rick sent you...."

"Rick did not send me; I sent myself. I am my own boss, and I issue my commands. I give myself assignments, and I report back to myself. Lobo Solitario," he said simply, with a smug look that was slightly amusing.

Bella frowned. Who calls himself a lone wolf? "If Rick did not send you, then why are you here?"

"Because I'm Rick's brother."

Bella looked fed up. She dropped her bag on the table and sat down. "How did you find me?"

"Sheer luck. The odds rolled the dice in my favor. Rick has been all over the city looking for you. Do you want him to lose his mind because of you? He cannot concentrate on anything, keeps blaming himself for your leaving."

She was silent for a while. "I had to leave," she replied.

"Why? You do not love him anymore?"

"No. that's not it." Her gaze flickered from him to the floor.

"Well then, what is it? I have all day to listen to you. That is why I'm here, to listen to you."

"I cannot tell you anything," she answered, shaking her head.

Drew sighed. Why did his stubborn brother have to marry a wife as stubborn as he is? "Listen. If you are afraid to cry, you don't have to be. I can even give you my shirt if you don't have a towel to dry your tears. But I want to know what is going on."

"I am not telling you anything, Drew. I'm not," she insisted.

Adamant. Drew noted. Very strong-willed. The Andersons were notorious for that. Two could play at this game. "I am not leaving this place until you tell me what is going on. Did Rick say something to you? Did he hurt you in any way?" He knew Rick could not, but he had to try.

"No. he did not say anything wrong, nor did it do anything wrong. Wait, why are we having this conversation?"

"Because Rick's life depends on it, and so does yours. Keep talking; I'm listening. Let me know when you need my shirt." Putting both elbows on the table, he folded his hands and rested his chin on them.

"I told you, Drew, I am not telling you anything."

"You can trust me. You can tell me everything."

Was he not listening? She bit her lip and tried again. "What if I don't?

"I will stalk you until you do," he said in a matter-of-fact tone.

"That is not even possible. You found me by sheer luck; you might not be so lucky next time."

"The odds are my best of friends; they will always be in my favor." He smiled impishly. He could keep poking at her shield until she gave in. He certainly would get her to talk. They could not continue that way, as Rick was probably still combing every familiar place he knew trying to find her.

"What makes you so sure? I do not have to tell you what I don't want to."

"You don't have to. I agree. But you will. If you walk out on me, I will find you. You can take that as a promise. Maybe I simply put a bug in your car."

The idea made her nervous. Such a simple trick would give him the chance to monitor her every move and whatever conversation she might have with anyone while being in the car. "You cannot do that."

"What if I already have?" he asked her leadingly.

"You have not," she argued.

"I would not be so sure if I were you," he replied, raising his brows mischievously, accompanied by a smirk. "Your car is outside. It is charcoal grey, isn't it? Other cars outside are either black, silver, or perhaps red. Yours isn't."

"You're just trying to coerce me into talking."

"Negative! I am trying to have a simple conversation which you obviously are avoiding, and I am beginning to wonder why." He thought his tone was enough to get her to talk.

"Because I don't want to talk about it. Don't you get it?"

"Listen, Bella, Rick has been my brother all his thirty-three years, and I know him well. Nothing, and I mean 'nothing' has ever rattled him this much. Now, if you are not bothered about the emotional torture and the psychological strain you are affecting him, which I presume you should be bothered about, I am. I am not happy seeing him in this state. Nothing scares a man more than losing the woman he loves dearly. If Rick has ever meant anything to you, and I mean ever, you would go back to him and find a way to mend whatever is wrong."

Bella was silent. She had not bargained for this. "The problem is not with Rick, the problem is with me!" she half yelled, shutting her eyes.

"What do you mean?" Drew replied, furrowing his brows.

She picked her bag and stood up. "I can't talk here."

Whether she talked there or somewhere else, the situation was a win-win for Drew. *I knew you'd talk,* he smiled inwardly. "We can go to my place; it's just across the street." She nodded, and he stood up.

Chapter Fifteen

Drew brewed two cups of coffee and placed one in front of Bella. He moved his easel to a corner of the room and pulled out an extra chair for himself. He sat on it and leaned backward, folding his arms. He could wait for as long as she wanted to gather her thoughts. He had waited this long; a few minutes would not hurt.

Sighing, Bella looked directly at him. "Why do I have to do this?"

Drew almost rolled his eyes. They had agreed, had they not? "Well, because I'm concerned about Rick and you as well. You'll be saving a lot of lives by doing this. Yours and his, maybe mine, and then there's our dad. That's a pretty long list if you ask me. I would appreciate it very much." There was another round of long silence, and Drew started to count to a hundred.

"Rick," she started, "I know I've hurt Rick a lot. Believe me, I never meant to push him away, but I had to. I just…I was scared of him. He had been under so much work pressure and had enough on his plate. And all I could think of was how long we had been married without succeeding in having children. In no way did I mean to hurt him; I just didn't understand myself, and as much as I might have wanted to reach out to him, I did not. I held back, and the more we pulled away from each other, the more I held back. Rick tried to make me happy, but…" the words caught in her throat. It was more than she could bear. "I love Rick; I really do."

"But something went wrong. What is it?" Drew asked, hoping it wasn't something serious.

"I started not feeling well and went to see a doctor to get tests done, and received a report… the report…." She could not complete her sentence. She broke down sobbing. Drew sat up straight and then looked around the room before going to his table drawer to pull out a box of tissues. He held it out to her, making her cry even more. He let her. She probably had been keeping in tears for too long now. He dropped the box on the side stool beside her chair and sat down again.

When she had quieted down a bit, he pursed his lips with a heavy sigh. "If you still need the shirt..." and pulled at its collar, making her chuckle a little.

She was hesitant; he could see it. Not only was she cautious, she truly appeared very scared, which made him even more curious about that unheard-of report that was tearing her and Rick apart.

"Drew. I have...I have cancer...bl...blood cancer." Her voice shook tremulously. "The doctor said... the report... oh, Rick, I'm so sorry." She was sobbing hysterically.

Drew froze in his chair in shock. "Holy mother of pastels." His mouth hung wide open for a while. "Why?" he asked silently. "Why did you not tell Rick?"

"I wanted to, I really did, but every time I tried, I got scared. So scared. It would tear him apart to find out. I thought if he knew I was going to die, he would never be able to get over it for the rest of his life," she said, her voice breaking.

The whole thing was now beginning to make sense. Bella was pushing Rick away deliberately. "You wanted him to hate you, isn't it?" She nodded yes, making him shake his head vigorously. It was amusing in the bitterest way possible. "It does not work that way. It will not. If you succeed in making rick hate you so much that you think he would want to forget about you. You can go to someplace he can never find you, which I presume is what you wanted to do; you will make Rick unable to forgive himself for his entire life when he finds out you were going through that much and you could not trust him enough to tell him," he listed, letting the words sink.

"He won't hate you; he will hate himself. He will blame himself forever. He will break apart completely, and it will take a long time to get him back to normal. That is what you are doing to Rick. You are not helping him by pushing him away; you are killing him. He is not handling the situation very well, Bella; he can't. Blood cancer can be treated; chemotherapy is an option unless it's beyond that stage. I do believe it's not. We can get other tests done to know how far it's gone. You don't have to undergo all this torment about your dying until you are sure of the outcome."

Bella was quiet. She had not thought about this whole thing from that point of view. She was only now realizing how much damage had been caused and how worse it could get. Very much worse. "Drew, I left so I could clear my head and think properly. Thanks for finding me. It's like a breath of fresh air in a sewer. I need to see Rick. Would you mind coming with me?"

"Absolutely not. I have been longing to see this day. It is so much of huge relief for me. Thank you, Bella." He smiled with hope and with love and a heart bursting with gratitude. "Let's go find Rick," he said as he rose from his chair.

Rick walked into his house and locked the door. Another fruitless search, was he thinking, and her number was still not going through. "Where in the planets are you, Bella? Where? Please come back to me. I really need you," he rasped, his voice devoid of strength and enthusiasm. His phone suddenly rang in his pocket. He brought it out and looked at the caller ID; it was Naveen.

"Hey," he said, expecting the question that would come next.

"Hello Rick, have you found her yet?"

"No luck. Have you?"

"Nope. No news from anyone, either. We'll keep looking. The weather forecast says there might be blizzards tonight. Stay warm, brother; she'll come to you."

"Aye, aye, captain," he replied to Naveen, then ended the call. He wished he could be as optimistic as his best friend. But where was optimism when bad news pitched a tent right in the middle of your house, blaring loud music with trombones and tubas and congas? Optimism simply was nowhere to be found. The temperature was dropping, and the air was chillier by the minute; the blizzard forecast might be true, he thought. He wondered if Bella was safe if she would stay warm like Naveen had told him to do. He walked to the heater and flicked it on, but nothing happened. He frowned in confusion and tried again, but it did not come on.

"It's supposed to start working." He grabbed its wire and traced it to the main socket, discovering that he had unplugged it the day before. He put it back in its socket, making it come on with an almost silent whirring sound. "That's better." He sank into a chair and stared fixedly at the wall clock; it was tending toward early evening. His eyes ached, and his eyelids drooped tiredly. He had had a sleepless night, drawing designs and scrunching up paper upon paper of rough sketches. It seemed to him like he had forgotten how to draw. His circles looked like an egg, and his straight lines were up and down like static wires; maybe it was his eyes after all. He drifted off to sleep in no time, the heat from the heater getting to him, pushing out the cold.

Drew rang the doorbell, waiting for a response. He had come alone; Bella had gotten a call from a friend of hers for something rather urgent, which she did not say anything about, and had to leave. He would have preferred to wait for her so they could go together, but after much thoughts, he decided to see Rick anyway. He could at least reassure him that he had found Bella.

He rang the doorbell again, losing count of how many times he had rung it. He looked at the doorknob and went by his instincts to try it. The door came open, to his pleasant surprise. Rick was fast asleep and had not even bothered to take off his clothes. He locked the door behind him and looked around the house. The atmosphere was almost crackling as it was very dry. He took a seat and studied Rick's outlook and demeanor for a moment. Judging from the way he was deep asleep, Drew figured that he might have been sleepless the night before. He shook his head and smiled. The dark clouds now have a silver lining, if only Rick would see it. Not really knowing what to do, he simply reclined into his chair, letting the warmth seep into his bones. It was getting very chilly outside, as he could smell a blizzard coming. He did not have to see the weather forecast to know that.

He wondered how long Bella would stay wherever she was. His phone buzzed, a signal of a text message. It was from Bella, and the content got him sprinting up from the chair. "Where are you? I'm at a bar, and my friend who needed my help is nowhere around. Some men are streaming in, and I have this strange feeling they'll stop me if I try to leave. Please come and get me out of here." He looked at Rick and decided it was best to wake him up, so they could go together.

He tapped him gently and then more firmly. "Hey," he said softly. "Hey, Rick, wake up." He shook him harder. Rick opened his eyes and looked around, trying to assess his surroundings and what was going on. A sharp ache ran through his head. He sat up and held it in his hands, trying to regain his composure.

"You are here?" he asked finally, his voice deep with sleep. How long had he been sleeping? A good one and a half hours. His forehead felt like it was on fire. He reclined himself back into his chair for a few seconds and then sat up again, getting more alert now. "Were you saying something?"

"Yes. This." Drew handed the phone over to Rick, hoping he was awake enough to read and comprehend the text message. When he shot up from the chair, Drew knew he was fully awake.

"What is going on exactly? You found her?"

"Yes. Sheer luck. Which is what I came to tell you. If you have any questions, save them until you see her. Meanwhile, let's get her out of that rat hole first. I only know of one bar that crawls with men like vile mice, and it is midtown. I think that is where she is."

"You have a mental catalog of all the bars in town? Who are you, Andrew Anderson?"

"An artist that seeks muses and inspiration." he grinned. "Are we leaving or discussing my knowledge of the city."

"You are crazy." Rick laughed in disbelief and grabbed his car keys from the table.

"If that is a compliment, then thanks. If it is not, double hearty thanks."

"A statement of fact."

"Can't be overemphasized. What's true is true," Drew stated as they left the house into the heart of the city.

Drew was right. The bar crawled with men whose life revolved around alcohol and gambling. The place was frequented by low-life people, making it a regular rounding-up spot for the police. Gambling was illegal, but no one cared, as they lived on it. And the police did not mind either. Cops simply chose perfectly unexpected times to storm the bar and just round everyone up into their vans.

Some of the men knew the innards of the prison-like the back of their hands; some jail time was not a deterrent for them. The government could screw itself for all they cared. As soon as they were out of prison, they found their way there. It was only a matter of time before they would be rounded up in an un-bailable arrest.

"What kind of a friend asks to meet here?" Drew shouted above the din of the noisy music that was coming from inside. Rick shrugged, indicating that he did not know.

"I have no idea. Bella surely does not keep friends like this," Rick shouted back.

"Gives me a reason to wonder why this had to be a venue, and then she refuses to show up. I smell a rat," Drew called out.

"Same here. Let us split up and look for her inside. Meet outside in ten minutes."

"Noted," Drew nodded, and then they went into the noise and reeking madness the bar contained.

Bella looked around furtively but not so much as to draw too much attention to her nervousness. It would simply make her an easy target. Someone collided against her from being pushed and staggered before regaining balance. He straightened and looked at her, sizing her up and contemplating whether to leave or stay. Seeing that he might probably want to stay, her nervousness heightened, and she suddenly felt queasy. *Where are you, Drew?* She looked around, but there was no familiar face except rowdy and somewhat rancorous actions that unnerved her. She so badly wanted to get out of there, but leaving without a male partner left her quite vulnerable.

"Hey. You look lonely, mind if I keep you company?" a stranger asked.

"I do mind. Thank you very much," she said, hoping he would not be such a pest and just leave.

"But what is such a dazzling beauty like you doing out here alone?" he pressed. Bella almost scoffed. Human-pest repellent was not such a bad idea after all, as there were people who truly needed it. Like when having this sort of fellow standing in front of her. Someone tapped the guy from behind. The stranger being a tall person, Bella could not see who it was.

"Get away from her," Rick said, his voice low and dangerous.

"Who do you think you are to tell me what to do?" the stranger asked, getting ready to start a fight with Rick.

"I am simply asking, get away from her," he repeated calmly.

"Whoa, you seem to be new around here. That is not how things work. I had dibs on her first, so you're the one who should get lost. She is mine."

Rick clucked his tongue at the guy's idiocy.

"Yours!" he said. "That is my wife, you idiot. My wife. Move aside," he said and shoved him to the side.

"If she is your wife...."

"What she is doing here is none of your business. Get lost." Rick spat in measured fury.

Bella was shocked or stunned, to say the least. How was Rick here? He had just saved her from a total pervert. Drew must have informed him, she finally thought, pleasantly surprised. "Rick!" He grabbed her by the wrist and pulled her to her feet.

"Let's get out of here. This place is a coven of criminals, and the police could be here any minute." He was right. No sooner than Drew found them outside and they left, the police arrived, blasting sirens loud enough to wake up the dead.

Rick dropped Drew at his apartment before heading home with Bella. The weather got worse, and the blizzard started blowing without mercy. Rick felt happiness. The snowstorm could rage on for days for all he cared, he had found his priceless treasure, and that was enough. The day would dawn with hope and a warm feeling in his heart that something new and pleasant was about to happen.

Sophia was fast asleep, her mouth hanging open slightly, making her look adorable. Naveen's eyes lingered at her face and then to her swollen belly. He gently rubbed circles on the belly and murmured, "Hey baby, your mom sleeps and eats like a panda these days, all thanks to you, but we can't wait for you to come into the world and fill ours with happiness. Know that we love you." He then leaned a little to plant a kiss on the belly and snuggled beside Sophia to sleep.

Chapter Sixteen

The snowstorm kept everyone indoors for a few days as it took a while to clear the heavy heaps of snow in order to free movement and ease off traffic. The sun seemed to erupt, smiling through the clouds as everyone was eager and happy to get out of their houses and into the streets.

"Hurry up, Sophia; we are going to be late," Naveen said from the bottom of the stairs as he was checking the time on his watch. "Are you done yet?"

"Almost!" she yelled back.

"And of all the days to be picky with what to wear," he muttered. She had turned her wardrobe inside out and still could not decide on what to wear. He tried helping, but it still did not work, and they were running late for the opening of Trent's restaurant. He skipped up the stairs and made it into the room where Sophia stood staring at an array of clothes. For someone who owned a boutique, she seemed to be at a loss of what to wear. She had added a little weight, and as the baby was taking up more stomach space, most of the clothes did not fit.

"I give up. I'm not going," she suddenly said, letting out a frustrated sigh as she sat down.

"Now, now, now. You cannot just conclude not to go. We can try one more time; there should be something that fits."

"Nothing fits," she said in exasperation.

"I'm sure something will."

"They are my clothes Naveen; I know they won't. You can go without me. Give my best wishes to Trent and Corinne, and take the present with you."

"I'm not leaving without you." He planted his hands firmly on his hips and did a quick scan again. Suddenly the lights came on. "Hold on; I have one for you." He pulled his side of the wardrobe open and brought out a wrapped, boxed present. "I was going to give this to you last week, but we all got up, stuck into looking for Bella. I hope you like it." He handed the gift over to Sophia, waiting for her response. He would simply get into bed and sleep if that did not fit either. He was not going to go out without her.

He watched Sophia open the present and unconsciously crossed his fingers. *Oh God, let it be a perfect size. We have been at this long enough.*

Sophia loved the dress just from seeing it. It was black velvet with silver trimmings and glittering little diamond studs; she couldn't wait to try it on.

Naveen heaved a sigh of relief. "It fits perfectly. Oh, I am so glad."

"It's beautiful. Thanks," Sophia replied. "You know just what I like and just what I need." She cooed softly and blew air gently against the back of his ear. She dodged before he could catch her.

"Are you flirting with me now?" he asked in amusement.

"Maybe," she winked as she finished getting dressed with whatever else was needed.

"We could fix a date for tonight," he replied, wiggling his eyebrows with a smug grin.

"Naughty." She swatted playfully at his hand as he brought it to her face. "We are late already; come on."

"Blame it on the clothes," he grinned as they stepped out of the room together.

Rick and Bella did not stay long at the restaurant opening ceremony, as they had a different destination in mind, which was the hospital. She had narrated everything to Rick, and Drew did not even have to be there. He was stupefied and found it very hard to believe. He wanted other tests done to be sure. He saw the report, but his gut feeling felt something was out of place. Bella could not possibly have cancer; it sounded outrageous. There had to be something else, maybe a mistake or a glitch in their lab procedures. He would not accept so easily his wife having blood cancer, to the point where he was ready to run tests in different hospitals and in other countries if need be.

"I don't believe it," he insisted, even while the paper stared him in the face. It was all psychological, whatever symptoms she felt. It had to be from fear and from believing the doctor, whom he presumed would have a reasonable explanation.

He took her hand and looked at her when the traffic light switched to red. "Are you alright?"

"Yes," she nodded. "Just nervous."

"You are fine, Bella. I know you are. We are going to confirm that," he said confidently, kissing the back of her hand before resuming his driving as the light switched back to green.

"You seem quite confident," she said.

"I got that from you. Remember when I was framed for something I did not do some years back? You were cocksure I did not do it, and that for me won the case, even more than the lawyer's efficient argument. Remember when I wanted to shelve taking up the steelworks corporation contract two years ago?"

"You were scared you would not be able to measure up to what they wanted. They were a picky and confused lot."

Rick nodded, remembering, "I could not have done it without you. I merged all their ideas into one more simple design, and they all loved it, all thanks to you. You did not give up on me, Bella, when I lost my first job. I'm not going to give up on you now either. We're seeing this through together. I'm not leaving your side again, not ever. I promise you that."

Bella's eyes were misty, glistening with gratitude. She was falling in love with Rick all over again. "Oh, Rick.

Thank you. Thank you for finding me. I felt so lonely, so lost without you."

"Thank you for coming back." He kissed her hands. "Drew found you; you could have decided not to come back. Thank you for doing so. Just don't ever scare me like this again."

"I promise," she said as they stepped out of the car into the hospital parking lot.

Doctor Sanders was looking up from the report belonging to the couple standing in front of Bella and Rick. For a moment, Bella was frightened that the couple might press charges against her; she had the feeling she might be in trouble. When the couple noticed that there had been a report mix-up, they had tried to contact Bella, but she had remained unreachable. The person who had the cancer report also bore the name Anderson. The elderly man had returned to the hospital, claiming he was given a wrong report. Not able to reach Bella to get his report, and with everything yet to be digitalized in that hospital, he had to undergo another series of tests, following which he had even started treatments, as he indeed had cancer. Bella wondered how to apologize to them, hoping they would be patient enough to hear her out.

"Mr. Anderson," she began. "My unreserved apologies to you and your wife for whatever misunderstanding this report might have caused. I'm deeply sorry."

"I don't understand," Rick said, sitting upright. He was now hoping there would be an underlying explanation.

"You see, there has been a report mix-up with your wife's and this gentleman who also goes by the name Anderson," Doctor Sanders replied. "Your wife was here, not feeling at her best, but we did not want to make any hasty conclusions. After asking her a few questions, she underwent a blood test and a urine test."

"And?" Rick asked.

"And the test results showed that your wife does not have cancer. Not a trace." Both Bella and Rick heaved in relief loud enough to hear each other. Rick was happier than a lark, and Bella felt freed of a burden. In the end, Rick was right, and Bella's fears were gone; she literally felt them evaporate.

"But…" Doctor Sanders started saying, short, living their exciting relief. "We detected a high level of HCG in her blood and urine, as well, and we discovered…."

"Discovered what?" Bella asked cautiously.

"Well, I'm glad to inform you that you're pregnant," Doctor Sanders said. She felt the words bounce off the wall and back at her. Both Bella and Rick seemed to be taking a while to process the good news. Were they not glad to hear that? She understood the gravity of the transition from thinking death-filled thoughts to hearing such news. She could only hope the slip-up would not call for trouble.

"What did you say?" Rick asked. If this was another report mix-up, he would certainly not take it lightly.

Doctor Sanders pulled out an envelope from under a folder and handed it to him. "This is your report. Your wife is going to be a mother as she tested positive. I apologize for the mix-up once again. It was a slip up on my part, and I shall take the blame."

Rick was not listening to the apology, and neither was his wife. If this report was true, then he accepted Doctor Sanders' apology wholeheartedly without even having to hear it.

"Is this true?" Bella asked, still scared to believe it but eager to accept it amidst other conflicting emotions. If it was true, then how about the symptoms she felt? Were they simply pregnancy symptoms she did not recognize, given she was swamped with other thoughts that beclouded hope? She had nausea, skin irritations, and slight bleeding, but none of it lit up a bulb in her mind. She had simply put herself through a lot, dragging Rick with her, and all the while, she had been pregnant? She started laughing at herself.

"If you need to be extra certain, you can, of course, do a home pregnancy test to be sure. When you do, please do not hesitate to check-in and register for prenatal appointments so that you and your baby's health can be monitored," Doctor Sanders offered.

Rick repeatedly nodded, having a continuous chuckle till he burst out laughing. "This is unbelievable. This is just amazing. Bella. This is great news. The storm is over, Bella. I told you that you were fine. Absolutely fine. You are not going anywhere. You're fine," he said again excitedly, rising from his seat and pulling her to her feet. He held her in a long embrace that made her forget what had happened. All those fears and worries had gone away, and now she was looking forward to a beautiful future. What a miracle life had been.

"I told you they would come when they're ready," he whispered, and she snickered in response.

"You were right. Thank you," she whispered back. Oblivious of the doctor's confused look or that of the nurse who had just opened the door to come inside and had stood to stare. Did they notice? Why would they care anyway? They had survived a storm, a boisterous blizzard, and they knew that thereon then, they could overcome any other hurricane.

Donald Anderson stood up with his walking stick and walked to the window. He had heard the news that Andrew was back in the city and wondered why none of his sons had come to see him. A part of him was filled with regret, for being the reason Drew had left ten years ago. If he had believed in either of his sons, he would not have to live so far apart from them today. He had lived every day, wishing he could rescind all his decisions and make new choices. Drew made a living from painting, the very thing he had been vehemently against. However, he eventually bought one of his paintings and hung it in his hallway, hoping that one day Drew would return to see it and realize that his father was proud of him. As he turned away from the window, a car wheeled into the premises and parked outside.

Drew looked at the edifice and its surrounding. The tarred driveway and the perfectly manicured lawns that remained, flanking either side. It was years he had been away from here. It was funny to see the same house he had grown up in look so strange to him now.

"How time flies," he said, facing Rick. "It's hard to believe I grew up here."

"We grew up here," Rick smiled slightly. Their childhood and early adulthood revolved around here. Baseball, chess, golf, taekwondo - every activity and skill they had acquired revolved around this mansion that they had become strangers to. They walked in silence until they reached the door. Rick rang the doorbell, waiting for a response from the intercom installed just beside it. There was no response, but the door was opened by one of the housekeepers, whom they did not recognize as they did not know him. Their father must have hired a new set of persons to attend to the house.

As they were walked into the residence, the hallway was echoed with their laughter and their memories. The decorations were the same; portraits still hung on the wall, souvenirs of every cherished moment, of every achievement, and of their growing up. Their dad had been there in every picture, with a broad smile that said how much he loved them and how much he cared. He had invested so much in seeing them grow, making sure they would be comfortable.

The housekeeper told them to wait while he went to call their dad. They did not have to tell the man who they were; he had seen their photos, and the resemblance was all too visible.

Drew moved closer to the wall to be sure he saw right. "Rick. Come and take a look at this."

"It's a painting," Rick said. "A beautiful one," he mused in admiration.

"I painted it," Drew dropped. "My name is right there at the lower left," Rick gaped in disbelief.

"Recognize it?" The baritone voice was still the same, not weathered by age or time. Both men turned around to look at their father. His voice had not aged, but his body had. He was looking much older, with wrinkles and deep worry lines woven across his face. He even had a walking stick. In the last picture Drew had of his father, he was still much on both feet by himself. Age was telling on him, coupled with an accumulation of the stress he had gone through in his younger years.

"Yes," Drew said. "I painted it."

"I know. That is why I bought it from my friend at the double amount he bought it from you," to which, Drew raised his eyebrows in questioning surprise.

"Why?" he asked, "double the price; that is a lot of money."

"Not too much to remind me of my son," he said simply. The old military tang was still there. "Boys." And the same mannerism of calling them, "it feels so good to see you again." He embraced them both, one after the other. Lingering in each embrace as though it would fill the gap of the years.

"My boys have grown. So much, I can barely recognize them," He said, smiling sadly. "Come. Let us catch up on old times." He then led the way back into the room he had been in before.

More paintings lined the wall in the room. It seemed like their father had suddenly taken a deep interest in arts, considering how, for a long time, he had not wanted to see a glimpse of color anywhere around.

He took a seat and motioned for them to sit as well. "You are not strangers; quit acting like some."

"How have you been, father?" Rick asked.

Donald smiled, his eyes glistening a little. "My little Rick has grown up. How else would I feel but happy? I have been happy. Hearing news about you both gave me joy, despite the distance and the lapse. Knowing that you are fulfilled makes me fulfilled," he said simply, closing his eyes. "I have been waiting for this day. Waiting for my sons. To tell them how proud I am of them and how much I've missed them." He breathed deeply and fell silent.

The two men looked at each other and wondered what next to say. The situation was awkward, and their father was not making it any better by talking like that. They knew very well he had not been as happy as he was saying. He had probably spent years wishing and being remorseful, which showed in his demeanor and his voice.

"Martha. She called me some days ago to ask how I have been. Are any of you boys hearing from her?"

Drew shrugged, and Rick shook his head. Neither of them had kept in touch with their mother for years. They never even felt she existed, nor did she. This was by far the oddest family reunion they had ever seen.

"How is she?" Drew asked.

"She should be doing fine," he answered, opening his eyes and looking at them. "Enough with the creepy act. I know the situation is awkward; let us add some spice to it, shall we?" he grinned, leaving them to wonder at the sudden transition. "Lobo Solitario. How have the years been on you? Found yourself a wife yet?"

Drew was taken aback. He took a while to convince himself that his dad had several unimaginable connections. He would not be surprised if he knew every country he had been in all these ten years. "No, I have not."

"You are not growing any younger, lad. I could find you one if you so wish."

Drew swallowed, and Rick held in his laughter. "Thanks, but I think I'll pass."

"Until your hair is as white as a sheet of snow on Christmas eve? You left this house ten years ago when you were twenty-five. Do the math. I'll be rooting for you in the New Year; let me know if you have trouble finding one."

Wives do not grow on trees, Father, he growled inwardly.

"Wipe that scowl off your face, and tell me something I don't know. Listen, lad. Don't take my words so hard to heart. Find yourself a woman you will love, and be sure to know that she loves you back. Some good woman who is not after your money," he said, with a tone that signaled he knew something beyond what he said.

"Tell us about our mother," Drew said, realizing that they did not know much about her. Each time they had asked him about her, he would simply tell them that she left, and that would be it.

Donald smiled. His sons were smart; they had taken after him in that regard. As he did, they could sense a person's unspoken words. "Martha," he said, his eyes dreamy and distant. "I am amused at how neither of you looks like her. I have to look at her picture to remember now what she looked like. She was beautiful, with short black hair like a pixie's and a smile that could captivate any man's heart. She was everything for me, everything I wanted. We made a promise that we would be there for each other, no matter what happened, and we were. That is until I lost my job a few weeks after Rick was born, and some man in a fancy car came and whisked her away right before my very eyes."

"Why did you not marry someone else?" Rick asked.

"I loved her, and I still love her as much. No one could fill that space," Donald answered, shaking his head.

Rick looked at Drew and then at Donald. "Why did she not come back?"

"She did not have to come back. She had all the luxury she wanted with her new husband. And she would not have had the gall to come back afterward. It took me years to build this empire; you boys know that. I singlehandedly raised you to be the best man you could be. So when Drew said he wanted to start painting, it sounded far from the pictures I had in my head. I wanted him to take over my business. No son of mine should go around mixing color like a rainbow. I, however, realized that he had found satisfaction in painting, and even more success than he would have ever had, had he taken over my business. And Rick, you were all over building blocks and drawing houses; you were leagues off what I wanted. Thanks for running off like you both did. It gave me enough time to think and to see the pictures in your hearts." He smiled and got up. "I want to show you both something."

Julie alighted from a taxi in front of the bookstore and went inside. She was coming to get wallpapers for her room and had learned they had just restocked. Perfect timing, she thought. She passed by the stationery section and down the books section when a book cover drew her attention. She walked over and picked it off the shelf.

"Nice. I have always wanted to read this book." She smiled and turned to continue when she saw someone staring in her direction. As he nodded slightly with a smile, she had to look back and around to make sure the greeting was for her. She smiled in return and continued her way toward the wallpapers and stickers section, wondering what that was all about.

"There is a whole lot of colors to choose from," she said, staring at the display of designs and patterns and pictures before her. She wanted to get a fresh look for her room before the Christmas holidays, which were only two weeks away. She needed something different from what she had and was simply awed by choices. Someone pulled out a medium-sized roll of white wallpaper, startling her. It was the same person who had greeted her earlier.

"Hi," he said with a broad smile. "Having trouble making a choice?"

"Yes," she replied.

"That is not a problem. I can help you with that. You can alternate plain and patterned wallpapers of similar colors and see if you like it."

She seemed to consider it for a moment. "That could work."

"What is your favorite color?"

"I don't want something I'm used to seeing, but it is mint green," Julie said, turning to look at the wallpapers again. "These are all nice, but it feels so hard to make a choice. It is as if my color was not here."

"Well, if you won't mind, I am an artist; I could paint you one," the man said, raising the roll of white wallpaper in his hand for effect. "You can get some of these, and I can paint anything you want on it. Graffiti, or watercolors, or an oil painting, or pastels, or colored pens."

"Is that what you do regularly?" she asked, suddenly liking the sound of the idea.

"Not exactly. I bought these for myself, but I can make an exception for you." He gestured toward the counter, "they get their things bought, you get wallpapers and a painting of your choice; everybody wins, everyone is happy," he grinned. "What do you say?"

Julie thought for a while and then looked at the book in her hand. She raised it for him to see. "Can you do this?"

"Absolutely," he nodded, taking the book from her to have a closer look at it. "Freidman Delgato," he mused. "You read his books too?"

"I'm a big fan. Do you also read his books?"

"I used to, back in college. I lost track after a while. Some crazy author he is," he nodded in admiration. "I can totally paint this. How wide is your room? Do you want a roof to floor covering?"

"Roof to the floor. It is about yay wide," she was pointing to a particular width of the wall of the store. "Not so much of a big room. Can you do it?"

"Hmm, if this painting stays on one side, how does the other side look?" He thought and snapped his fingers in a eureka fashion. "I've got it."

"What do you have in mind?"

"Something magical. I'm sure you are going to love it. By the way, my name is Drew. Drew Anderson," he said, extending his hand.

"Julie Bill. It's a pleasure meeting you."

"The pleasure is all mine." He pulled out another roll of white wallpaper and waved it. "When do we start?"

"Tomorrow. You can give me your number, and I will text you my address."

"Not a problem," he said with a smile that hid his curiosity.

Whether Drew believed in sparks or not, he did not know, but he knew there was something about this newly found friend that he needed to find out.

Everything was changing. The cold and wet weather was saying its goodbyes so people could welcome Spring, with sunny afternoons and the aroma of cherry blossoms in the air. Cupid seemed to be working way too hard these days, hitting as many hearts as he could and smiling as it saw love floating in the air, mixed with the scent of cherry blossom.

Chapter Seventeen

Cleo opened the door and came out with a watering can for the plants in the garden that she was growing at the side of the house. She had barely left the porch when a motorbike came up the driveway and stopped just in front of her home. The rider had a heavy-looking backpack and took off his helmet before he alighted from the bike. She stood still, wondering who the stranger was and what he wanted. She waited as he covered the little distance between them.

"Good afternoon, ma'am," he said cheerfully.

"Good afternoon. How may I help you?" she asked politely.

"Does Julie Bill live here?" Drew asked.

"Yes, she does. You are looking for her?"

"Yes. I have an appointment with her. My name is Drew."

"Oh, she mentioned you were coming. Alright, hold on, I will be back shortly." She dropped the watering can and went back inside.

Drew put his hands in his pocket and waited.

"Drew, hi. You are here," Julie said as she came out.

"Am I late?" he asked cautiously.

"No, you are just in time. Come on in," she replied, opening the door wider to allow him to come inside. "My room is upstairs, right this way."

The room was originally painted white, and the former wallpaper had been peeled off. Drew noticed she had moved all the furniture to the center of the room, including her bed and a dressing table. No pictures were hanging on the walls either.

"Makes my work easy," he mused. "How did you move all these?"

"Dad helped me move them this morning. So, where do we start?" she asked, bubbling with excitement. For a twenty-four-year-old, she had a rather boisterous and lively attitude.

Confusion flecked Drew's face. "We?" When did this become a 'we' job? he replied. He was supposed to be the painter.

"Yes, I want to help you. The room is fairly big. My sister and I used to do it before she got married. We have been changing our room wallpapers a few weeks before Christmas every year since childhood, and we always did it together," she said reflectively.

"You miss her, don't you?"

"Very much. Do you have any siblings?" she asked suddenly.

An inquisitive question, he noted. "I have a brother. We look so much alike," he said, dropping his backpack to the ground to open it.

"Really? I can imagine."

"Yep. Same hair, same eyes, same smile, but not the same life," he said, bringing out his equipment one piece after the other.

"What does he do?" Julie asked.

"He is an… architect," Drew replied slowly, holding up a can of spray paint and making sure he had picked the right color.

"Sounds fascinating. I would like to meet him one day. It would be nice to see you stand beside your look alike."

"What about you? What do you do?" Drew asked, lining up cans of spray paints and different sizes of brushes.

"I'm rounding up my computer engineering course in college. I work with the software development unit back at the college where I am attending, and I am also an intern with a company that deals with computer vision and robotics. That is what I intend to specialize in after college. Visual sensing technology."

Drew stared at her for a long while. She did not look anything like someone who was involved with computers. He would have believed her had she mentioned anything else but that. She spewed brilliance in the few seconds she spoke. "Now that is something interesting. I am quite surprised and impressed."

"Thank you," she said with a grin. "So, did you study arts in college?"

"Nope. I studied economics." Drew brought out a meter rule and held it out to her. "Hold this for me, will you?" He held the tape and pulled it while walking backward. "I studied economics at the University of Chicago, second best graduating student. Top of the pop, the face of the class."

Julie gaped and looked at the paints and brushes. "This certainly does not look like economics."

"You mean what I do? Well, passion is one thing; the norm is another. You do not look like a computer genius yourself. Calculations and dead man's theories? Not my style. I work with colors; that is my breathing space," He chuckled.

Julie studied him for a moment. He was an interesting person, quite enigmatic, but still very simple. "You know, I can't say why we met, but I think we are going to be good friends."

"Ditto," he grinned. "Alright, enough talking, let's get serious." He brought out his apron and strapped it on. He always carried an extra, so he gave it to her. "You will need this."

"Thanks," she said. "Hey, if I spray one of these on your hair, would it come off?" she picked up a can of spray paint as he spread out the wallpaper.

Drew's look was laughable. His hair? Why not hers? "How about we try it on yours and see if it comes off.

I can guarantee you it is not going to come off. You can get a whole jar of shampoo and wear it as a hat, and it still would not come off."

"It would not hurt to try," She moved toward him with the can.

"Keep that thing away from me. Keep it…" he dodged and caught the can before she could spray it. "Graffiti paint, not for my hair," he said.

"Alright." She put up her hands in mock surrender. She looked at him as he set to work with all concentration and fluid skillfulness. She was beginning to like this artist; she only wondered how much.

"Time will tell," she thought.

"I can tell you now; you sure like him a lot," her heart whispered, and she shushed it at once.

Four months later.

Sophia was stirring in the middle of the night, feeling uncomfortable and tired. She flicked the bed lights on and looked around. She sat up and looked at Naveen, fast asleep. She shifted quietly from the bed, and her hand touched a wet patch on it. She felt it again to be sure. Her water had broken, and she did not know how long that had been because she slept early as the contractions were setting in. She tapped Naveen on the shoulder several times before he woke up, feeling very groggy.

"What time is it?" he asked, sounding extremely sleepy.

"I do not know. I did not check. Naveen, the baby." she said.

The sleep vanished from his eyes. "What?"

"The baby," she said, nodding slowly and repeatedly.

"Is she coming?" He sat up and looked around, not knowing what to do. She had had false labor about two weeks ago, but this time it seemed real. "I need to find my car keys."

Seeing him search the odd places for his keys in a frantic frenzy was funny, and she could not help giggling. She was not even as panicky as he was.

"Calm down, Naveen. You need to dress up first."

"Calm down? The baby is on its way, and you want me to calm down? How are you even so calm?" he asked.

"You know your keys are not in the flower vase, so do not look in there. If you are not calm, you are not going to find them."

She suddenly winced and held her breath for a while before releasing it slowly. "One... two... three..." she whispered, making Naveen panic even further.

"Oh God, where are these keys?" He snagged a sweatshirt from his wardrobe and began to put it on while checking under the pillows.

"You are wearing your shirt inside out," Sophia said with a slight chuckle. He paused and looked at it and then at her.

"Oh no," he said, letting out an exasperated sigh. She was laughing ever so calmly, of all the things to do in this situation, laughing! He pulled out the pair of jeans trousers he had worn earlier in the day, and his keys fell out. "Could you not say you were here?" he said to the keys as he picked them up.

"Keys, do not talk," Sophia said.

"I know that," he said, pulling open her side of the wardrobe. "This... no... not this either... this... don't think so..."

"What are you doing?"

"Finding you a dress," he replied without looking back. "This should do, I hope. Would this fit?" He was holding one up for her to see.

"I do not like the color."

"I am not talking about the color." He watched her squeeze; her eyes shut again, and his apprehension rose. "Naveen, you chicken of a man, your wife is calm, and you are acting as if you were the one in labor," he said to himself.

When she had finally calmed down, she looked up at him and said the time gap was reduced by at least two minutes. They needed to get to the hospital soon. "Do I have to wear anything? It feels so hot in here."

Naveen paused before responding. "Yes, you have to wear a dress, please put it on so we can leave now," he said slowly and measuredly while handing the cloth to her.

"The bag is in the nursery."

"Great. Thanks, I was about to ask. I will be right back." he said and hurried out of the room.

She was dressed before he could return, to which he heaved a sigh of relief.

"Can you walk?" he asked. Sophia raised her eyebrows as if to ask a question.

"Absolutely. I am fine Naveen, I am fine."

"That is as clear as the sun at midnight. Who are you kidding? Come on, let's get you to the doctor," he said, helping her up. "Are you sure you can walk?"

"Can you carry me down the stairs?" she teased.

"You know I can."

"I told you I could walk," she said and started slowly walking out of the room.

"Great. That's a relief," he huffed and followed her.

She paused halfway down the stairs, stopping to catch her breath.

"Sophia …"

"I am fine," she gasped faintly.

"No, you are not."

"It is called labor Naveen, contractions. They are just getting closer, about eight minutes apart, or thereabouts."

"The closer they get, the faster we have to get you to the hospital."

"Can I drive?" she asked.

"Really now? Stop kidding. You can't even fit behind the wheel. Are you good to walk?"

"Yes. I think so."

"Good." He helped her down the stairs and dropped a note for Frances before they left the house.

Rick bounced up the stairs into the hospital; if only he could fly, was he saying to himself. He had gotten Naveen's text out of the blues and had raced down after a long session of trying to convince Bella not to come along.

She was due in three months, and he did not want any tension or shock to cause something they would not be prepared for. He found Julie and Cleo waiting already. George was out of town; else, he would have been there.

"Hi. How is it going?" he asked.

"Not too long now. She wants a natural delivery, so it might take a while. Naveen is there with her; the doctors did not want too many people in there," Cleo explained.

"Oh." he nodded.

Julie stood up to stretch, "I called Drew. He should be here soon," she said. Four months had been enough time for Drew to see that she was all he wanted and enough time for her to figure out that she did not want to be with anyone else but him, not minding that he was thirty-five and she was twenty-four.

"He felt like family the first day he came with his backpack to our house," her mother had said, and even George agreed. It was easy as he was free-spirited and friendly. Moreover, George was once a student at the University of Chicago and also loved to paint. Prospective son-in-law checklist, he had straight A's.

As for Donald, he was completely tickled, as Julie had a very lively attitude and was good with computer technology; he embraced her with open arms.

"Drew, my boy, you have done very well for yourself. I am very proud of you," he had said when they had both gone visiting.

It was a big surprise for Naveen, Rick, and Sophia, on the other hand, when they were told about Julie and Drew. Rick had laughed till his sides hurt, stopped, and then started another round of laughter.

"Julie? Sophia's sister? How on earth did you two meet and hit it off?" he asked with surprise. "Wait till Naveen hears about this; I can't wait to see the look on his face. Congratulations brother. You have successfully merged our families; there is no other way to explain it."

Drew shrugged with a smile. "I can't explain it either, but I do know I have found my woman," he said.

The delivery room door opened about an hour later, and they all stood up at once.

"How is she?" Cleo asked.

"She's perfectly fine. It is a girl. My hearty congratulations. She is a strong woman for a first-timer," the doctor replied cheerfully.

Cleo breathed in relief. "That is great news. Thank you, doctor."

"Can we see her now?" Julie put in.

"In a few minutes. Just hold on a little longer. The nurse will let you know when you can," he said. "I'll take your leave."

"Yes, please." Cleo stepped aside for him to leave.

The house was quite full and quite lively. Frances beamed with joy as she attended to the people that came in with their wishes. They were friends, acquaintances, and colleagues.

"I think she looks like Sophia," Rick said.

"No, your eyes are getting old; she looks like me." Naveen protested.

"Really? How so?" Rick asked.

"Well, she has my eyes," Naveen started.

"And Sophia's face," Rick responded.

"But with my hair."

"You both have the same hair color."

"No, we do not...."

Julie rolled her eyes. "And here they go again. I think she looks like mom, alright? That should settle it. She takes after her grandmother. Quit arguing and give my ears a break."

Frances came into the room with a little package. "Naveen, this just arrived for you. It says to hand it over to you specifically."

"Let me see it. Was it a postman?" he asked.

"Yes. I already signed, and he left."

"Thanks, mother," Naveen said. The words caught her by surprise. "You have been more than just a housekeeper. You have been in the place of my mother. Thanks for raising me like your own son Frances. I owe you so much," he said, standing up to embrace her.

"I never had a son, but I had the joy of raising you and your brother. I wish he were here and your father as well," she said, her voice tremulous.

"They are in a better place, and I'm sure dad thanks you every day for all you have done." He smiled and proceeded to open the package. He whistled in surprise, and a pleasant smile played across his face. "You will not believe this," he said.

"Who is it from?" Sophia asked.

"It is a wedding invitation from Ryan and Drizella."

"No way," Rick said. "Whoa, I did not see that one coming. Drizella's actions turn out to be a blessing in disguise. Now that is some big news."

"Looks like the inspector found a gem as well. Was he not supposed to be on duty?" Julie asked, causing them to laugh.

Sophia looked at the invitation card and felt her heart warm up. There was a letter attached to it. "Thanks for believing in me, Sophia. I would not be here without you. I owe big. Love, Drizella."

"Thank you, Naveen," she said.

"What for?" he asked, slightly confused.

"For removing your charges against her," Sophia replied.

"You are the one who convinced me, so you should be getting the thanks. You saw the changes, and you made me see it."

"Rick, I think we should excuse them and let them have their moment," Julie said with a teasing note.

"I agree. I will be right outside with my wife," Rick said, taking exaggerated long strides out of the room.

"Cheerio," Julie said, following suit.

Frances chuckled and shook her head. "Not to worry, I am just on my way out. Let me know if you need anything," she said, leaving the room as well.

There was a lingering silence for a while before Naveen spoke. "What was that all about?"

"I have no idea," Sophia shrugged.

Naveen sat beside her and held her in a side embrace. "I'm glad for so many reasons. I got so many gifts last year, and you were the greatest of them all. Thanks for coming into my life Sophia."

She turned her head so she could look at him. "Is there a rule that says I must get all the credit? I should thank you as well for coming for me each time I ran away."

"You were good at doing that," he chuckled.

"I'm not leaving again. Not today, and not ever," she said, and the words stayed with a resonance that echoed in his heart forever.

Epilogue

The sun was shining brightly through the clouds, and so was everybody's smile as Drizella got ready to throw her bouquet for the second time. Julie had not seen it coming as she was about to pick a call. The bouquet fell softly against her face, and she caught it before it reached the ground in reflex. She was standing up to applause and getting a cheeky grin from Drew.

"When is the date?" he asked, tucking a loose strand of hair behind her ear.

"Next summer," she grinned as she went to embrace Drizella.

"You caught my bouquet!" Drizella piqued in excitement.

"I caught your bouquet!" she said, with a matching excitement. "Congratulations to both of you."

"And to you too," Ryan said. "I'm rooting for you and Drew."

"Everyone is, especially dad," Rick joined in. "And here he comes."

Donald smiled and raised his walking stick briefly. "From the moment I saw you, I just knew I wanted you in my family. From now on, we will speed up wedding preparations double time. Right Drew?" did he say, turning to him.

"Absolutely."

As they gathered for a photo shoot, the air reeked of memories, of the fights they had won, of the storms they had weathered, of the good moments they had enjoyed, of the battles they had withstood each of them and together as one, of the lessons learned. It reeked of promises, and strength, and hope, and love, and the assurance that family went beyond four walls and that they were each other's strength. They knew that they could weather any storm and boisterous blizzards as long as they lived. Their smiles held

the confidence that they could face Hamish and track him

down once again if he ever came back in their life, which

they were convinced he was not. They would stay even if

everything said leave. They would learn to trust one

another's gut feelings and decisions. They would always

give love a chance every time it came about, and if

anything was threatening their bonding, they would not let

it seep in with the slightest trickle—not today, and not ever.

www.ingramcontent.com/pod-product-compliance
Lightning Source LLC
Chambersburg PA
CBHW020414030726
47495CB00006B/1499